Henry Cecil was the pseudonym _____, Cecil
Leon. He was born in Norwood Green Rectory, near
London, England in 1902. He studied at Cambridge
where he edited an undergraduate magazine and wrote a
Footlights May Week production. Called to the bar in
1923, he served with the British Army during the Second
World War. While in the Middle East with his battalion he
used to entertain the troops with a serial story each
evening. This formed the basis of his first book, *Full Circle*.
He was appointed a County Court Judge in 1949 and held
that position until 1967. The law and the circumstances
which surround it were the source of his many novels,
plays, and short stories. His books are works of great
comic genius with unpredictable twists of plot which
highlight the often absurd workings of the English legal
system. He died in 1976.

THE WANTED MAN

by

Henry Cecil

HOUSE OF
STRATUS

This edition published in 2000 by House of Stratus, an imprint of
Stratus Holdings plc, 24c Old Burlington Street, London, W1X 1RL, UK.

www.houseofstratus.com

Typeset, printed and bound by House of Stratus.

A catalogue record for this book is available from the British Library.

ISBN 1-84232-068-8

Contents

Author's Note

This novel is based upon a short story
and a radio play of the same name
which I wrote a few years ago.

CHAPTER ONE

The Newcomer

'Your wife is a mocker,' said the vicar, the Reverend Harvey Bagshot, to the commander, 'and whosoever is deceived thereby is not wise.'

'I thought that was wine,' said the judge.

'Wives too, sometimes,' said the vicar.

'Well, it was a jolly good game anyway,' said the judge. 'I had all the luck.'

Commander George Blinkhorn RN, Retd, and His Honour Judge Herbert Ward were good friends. They were also the best of opponents and the worst of partners. At croquet, that is. What they would have been like together in real war will never be known. The judge had been in the Army and they had never taken part in the same combined operation. But if their behaviour at croquet is any guide, the proverbial order, counterorder and disorder might well have prevailed. As opponents each of them always played hard to win, regularly gibed at the other between the turns, cheered his good shots and commiserated with his mistakes. The judge did not mind whether the ten bob (you couldn't bet someone fifty new pence) which they wagered on every game was won or lost. The commander did mind but it was pride, not meanness. The honesty of their play would have been a lesson to politicians and a few lawyers.

But when they partnered one another it was a very different story. Before the game began this sort of dialogue would take place.

'Look, George,' the judge would say, 'let's make a pact. I'll take your advice the first time if you'll take my advice the next.' This was always agreed, but who was to decide which was the 'next' time? Under the rules of croquet after the first four turns each side may play whichever of its balls it chooses. Naturally the ball in the better position is chosen. But which is in the better position? And who is to decide that matter? Theoretically one partner could play the ball a dozen or more times in succession. Very hard on the other if he didn't agree with the strategy.

'Give me patience,' the commander would begin.

'You're not on your beastly quarterdeck now,' the judge would say.

'You're not in your beastly police court.'

'Trouble between friends?' the vicar would enquire.

'You've never partnered Bertie,' the commander would say.

'I'm never allowed to. I'm too good,' the vicar would reply with unchristian immodesty.

On this occasion until shortly before the arrival of the vicar the commander's wife, Elizabeth, had been happily engaged in her favourite corner of the garden where there were always weeds to be dug up and rearrangements to be made. But she listened for the croquet balls to stop clicking, which would be the sign for her to go and make the tea. The clicking stopped just before the vicar arrived and so Elizabeth left her weeds and rearrangements, went to the kitchen, made the tea and came out with it.

The commander and the judge had returned from the croquet lawn just as the vicar came in. After they had greeted one another Elizabeth asked who'd won. She always asked this even if she could see by his face that her husband had lost. It was a choice of evils. If she didn't ask, she might be accused of lack of interest and that would be worse.

'Bertie won,' said the commander.

'I expect it was very close,' said his wife.

'By twenty points.'

'I don't suppose it reflected the run of the play,' said Elizabeth. 'It must have been pretty close really.'

It was then that the vicar made his adaptation from the Book of Proverbs.

'By the way,' said the commander, 'did you know that they've sold next door at last?'

'I bet they had to come down in price,' said the judge. 'What was it they were asking for it? Twenty thousand, wasn't it? And with only one bathroom.'

'D'you know who's bought it?'

'I've no idea.'

'As a matter of fact,' said a strange voice, 'I have.'

They all looked at the stranger who had come into the garden unnoticed.

'Do forgive me barging in like this. My name is Partridge, Donald Partridge. And I'd be terribly grateful if you'd tell me where the nearest police station is. The telephone isn't on yet in my house.'

'You haven't had a burglary already, have you?'

'Rather worse,' said Mr Partridge. 'Somebody has just shot at me.'

'No! D'you know who?'

'No. That's what's so odd. I was in the orchard when suddenly there was a shot. I looked round but couldn't see

3

anyone. Five minutes later there was another. It must have been very close because I could smell it.'

The judge laughed. 'I think we can save you a visit to the local police. It was me.'

'What *are* you talking about, Bertie?' said Elizabeth. 'You've been here all the time.'

'*Qui facit per aliud facit per se,*' said the judge.

'He means,' said the vicar, 'that someone else did it on his behalf.'

'I said *aliud*, Harvey. Not *alium*,' said the judge. Some*thing* else did it for me. I saw that the birds were playing merry hell with the trees. The last owner used to give us some of his fruit, so just in case the new owner was likely to be as generous I put up a few bird scarers. Sorry they've given you a fright. I didn't know you'd come in yet.'

'Well, I'm not quite in yet. It'll be another few days. But thank you very much for looking after the orchard. Please help yourself to the fruit whenever you like. There's far more than we shall be able to eat.'

'The last people used to market it.'

'Oh, I couldn't be bothered,' said Mr Partridge. 'But I mustn't interrupt you. I shouldn't have come in if I hadn't thought someone was trying to kill me.'

'Do stay and have some tea,' said Elizabeth.

'I'd be imposing.'

'Certainly not. I insist. Don't we, George?'

'It's very, very kind,' said Mr Partridge. 'I'll accept gladly. I suppose this is or was on the Winchcombe estate.'

'Yes,' said the commander, 'the whole of Little Bacon at one time belonged to it.'

Little Bacon, the village near which the commander and the judge and now Mr Partridge lived was an ideal retreat. Mrs Winchcombe, who still owned much of the land in the neighbourhood, which she had inherited from her first husband, kept a pedigree dairy herd, several horses and dogs and a husband. Henry Winchcombe, like the horses and dogs had been well trained. His wife never actually said to him, as she said to the dogs, 'Sit', but a look in her eyes or a motion of her head usually indicated to him what he was to do next. And he did it. Nobody could have called him henpecked because the pecks left no wounds. He enjoyed being kept by his wife, body and soul. He was a retired schoolmaster with a very small pension but he was not a schoolmaster who wanted to teach anybody except the boys and girls in his school. He was forty when he married for the first time. Mrs Winchcombe, on the other hand, had been married twice before. She had been fond of each of her husbands but her fondness in no way prevented her from acquiring another.

Her cousin by marriage, Henry Winchcombe, was the obvious choice for the third occasion. He had invited her to marry him twice before, but each time she had preferred someone else. The third time, she decided to give Henry a chance and he took it gratefully.

Husbands were as necessary to Mrs Winchcombe as dogs and horses. She was kind to them all but they had to do what they were told and on the whole the husbands were only supposed to speak when they were spoken to. Mrs Winchcombe hated desultory conversation. Conversely, she always encouraged people to talk on subjects in which they were really well versed. The one subject upon which Henry Winchcombe was allowed to speak was wine. The fact that his knowledge of burgundies and clarets was unrivalled in the neighbourhood of Little Bacon did not mean very much because there were no real connoisseurs in that area. But Henry could have held his own on those two particular subjects with most of the journalists who write about wine. Fortunately for him his wife's means enabled him to keep an exceptionally good cellar and even those who knew very little about the subject very much enjoyed the dinners at Broadway House where the Winchcombes lived.

Mrs Winchcombe was in command of these dinners as she was in command of her whole household. She liked the talk of experts and for the most part would not allow any other conversation at the table. The commander was therefore only allowed to talk about the navy, the judge about the law and the vicar about the church and so on. Every now and then, however, Mrs Winchcombe discovered that one of her neighbours was an expert on something else. For example, the judge knew a good deal about monumental brasses, while the vicar had a profound knowledge of music. It was in this way that Mrs Winchcombe added to her store of knowledge which otherwise would have been limited to that of husbandry in all senses of the word.

The nearest town to Little Bacon was Brinton, ten miles away. Few motorists invaded Little Bacon or the neighbourhood, as there was no public house and not even a church. The church was two miles away at Mildon. In consequence anyone whose pleasures were listening to music, reading, seeing his friends or looking at the countryside could live in Little Bacon very happily for the rest of his life. It was an ideal place for such a person to retire to, as it was for anyone tired of too much noise, too many people and too much happening.

Almost all the houses near Little Bacon had at one time or another been bought from the Winchcombe Estate. Mrs Winchcombe's estate manager was very popular in the neighbourhood, mainly because he was so helpful to everyone. With Mrs Winchcombe's full consent he was somewhat prodigal with her assets. Mrs Winchcombe was tidy minded and she liked the country around her to be tidy. Accordingly when a new gate or a new fence or even a new wall would make the place look better, if the Winchcombe Estate did not actually provide it, it went a long way towards doing so. In consequence there was no better kept part of the country in England.

The last occupier of the house which Mr Partridge had bought had been a solicitor whose wife could never settle, and after ten years of changing the drawing room into a studio and the studio back again into a drawing room, of laying down a tennis court and a croquet lawn and then changing them into a large swimming pool – and back, the Chessingtons left to do the same again in some other part of the country. Fortunately for Mr Partridge he arrived just after they had done away with the swimming pool and reinstated the tennis and croquet lawns. Mr Partridge hated water and couldn't swim. On the other hand he enjoyed playing tennis badly and he was prepared to do the same at croquet.

CHAPTER TWO

Beginning of a Sentence

Just about six months before Mr Partridge joined the community at Little Bacon, Mr Justice Boynes was considering what sentences to pass on men who had been guilty of a huge conspiracy to rob a bank. Possibly the word 'huge' is inappropriate because the amounts now stolen from railway trains and banks and others are so astronomic (in a recent bank raid it was suggested that about five million pounds in money or goods were stolen) that anything under a million pounds might be considered as comparatively trivial. In estimating the net gain to the robbers it must also be remembered that the expense of these operations is considerable. Experts of different kinds have to be employed and a large number of people usually take part in the operation. They must, of course, be suitably rewarded. In most cases the object of those taking part is to gain sufficient from the one enterprise to enable themselves to live happily ever after without recourse to crime or, worse still, work.

Criminals for the most part do not expect to be caught. They are incurable optimists. Even men with eight previous convictions, when they start on their evening's work, do not expect that there will be a ninth. On the other hand, most of those engaged on really big robberies calculate that, even if they are caught, the operation will be worthwhile. At the moment criminals seldom stay in prison for more than ten or twelve years at the most, and a man of thirty who has been in prison before will reconcile himself to, say, twelve years' imprisonment if he knows that when he comes out he will only have to go to a certain safe deposit to find a hundred thousand used pound notes waiting for him. An Act has been passed by Parliament providing that these men shall be made bankrupt and liable to hand over their ill-gotten gains. They are liable to hand over their ill-gotten gains, whether they are made bankrupt or not. But the trouble is that gains, though ill gotten, can be well hid and the probability is that in most cases where the robbery is a large one the effect of bankruptcy on the offender will merely be to add a slight stigma to a reputation which a sentence of twelve years' imprisonment will have somewhat tarnished.

If there are twenty people involved in the criminal enterprise and the amount expected to be obtained is about a million pounds, this will mean only fifty thousand pounds each or rather less after the expenses of the enterprise have been deducted. Such a sum may be sufficient to support a man whose life is not centred on a variety of women, cars and horses. But probably many of them consider that years of imprisonment must be compensated for by a continuous round of wild gaiety. It is easy enough to dispose of the bulk of fifty thousand pounds in this way. Accordingly, one can conceive a man, when offered a part in such an enterprise, turning it down on the ground that fifty thousand pounds is not enough. Many criminals today are probably highly sophisticated. And one could imagine Mr X working it out thoughtfully and logically. £20,000, say, to be used for riotous living to make up for the years of imprisonment and the balance to be used for a comfortable work free life thereafter. £30,000 would not be enough for this purpose. So the minimum is a hundred thousand pounds.

There is one way to give real discouragement to such people, namely the imposition of sentences of imprisonment for the rest of their lives, unless and until it is certified by some suitable body that it is safe to release them. Although many of these men do not want to use unnecessary violence the amount at stake is so large and the idea of being caught with the booty on him is so intolerable that it is difficult to think that the average robber would not use violence to evade arrest. If it became known that violent robbers would never be released except when certified safe it might do a little to discourage such enterprises. But, of course, the best discouragement is to have a police force of double the size of the present force.

In the case before Mr Justice Boynes twelve men were involved and the amount stolen was two and a half million pounds. None of it had been recovered, not even the ten per cent which the Great Train robbers left behind. This was a matter which naturally troubled the judge a good deal. He had considered the various matters just referred to and he tried to work out the best course for him to take in the interests of the public. He felt that it was his duty to do what he could to assist in the recovery of the money but he had little confidence that he would be successful. It was fairly well established that the ringleader was a man called John Gladstone. According to the police Gladstone was a man with no previous convictions, though Chief Superintendent Beales, the officer in charge of the case, gently suggested that he was suspected of being the brain behind several previous crimes.

'He is an educated man,' said the superintendent, 'and he tells me that he was originally intended to go in for the law, but I have been unable to confirm this. He is aged 48, he says that he is married but that his wife left him some years ago and he does not know her whereabouts. He lives in a comfortably furnished flat for which he pays a rent of £1,250 per annum. I have been quite unable to discover any honest way in which he has been able to pay his rent. He has not given me particulars of any employment or work which he has undertaken in the past years. The rent is not in arrear. He, like all the others, refused to give me any particulars which will enable me to trace the money stolen or any part of it.'

'Do you wish to cross-examine, Mr Jenkins?' asked the judge of defending counsel.

'If your lordship pleases. Superintendent, you are suggesting that my client has been living on the proceeds of crime?'

'I am.'

'Have you any evidence of this?'

'Only that he lives in a comparatively, expensive way, as far as I can see he has no debts and – '

'Except to the bank,' interrupted the judge.

'Quite so, my lord,' said the superintendent. 'I should have said that he has no *other* debts, my lord, but, as he is not prepared to tell me how he is able to pay his way – '

'You assume the worst,' put in Mr Jenkins.

'If you like to put it that way,' said the superintendent.

'Has it occurred to you,' asked Mr Jenkins, 'that he might be kept by a woman and doesn't like to say so?'

'Are those your instructions, Mr Jenkins?' asked the judge.

'No, my lord, I was merely suggesting to the superintendent an alternative way in which the accused might have been living.'

'Why not suggest the way in which he is in fact living, Mr Jenkins?' said the judge. 'Your client knows and is quite capable of instructing you in the matter.'

'If your lordship pleases,' said Mr Jenkins.

'If it's any help to you,' said the judge, 'I am going to treat your client as a man who has not previously broken the criminal law. He has no previous convictions against him and he is therefore entitled to be so treated.'

'Then,' said counsel. 'I won't ask the superintendent any further questions.'

'Well, Mr Jenkins,' asked the judge. 'What do you want me to say on behalf of Mr Gladstone in mitigation? He has pleaded guilty to a very grave theft and there appears to be little doubt that he is the ringleader.'

'In spite of that, my lord,' said counsel, 'I have a great deal to say on his behalf. I hope your lordship will hear me with patience.'

'I hope I always listen to counsel with patience.'

'I know your lordship does.'

'Then I can't quite see why you mentioned the subject.'

'I apologise, my lord,' said counsel. 'It was foolish of me. Now, my lord, the first thing I want to say on behalf of my client is this. I can't dispute that he has pleaded guilty to a very serious crime, but I do ask your lordship to bear in mind that instead of putting the prosecution to the vast expense of proving his guilt in this court and instead of going into the witness box and committing perjury and instead of conspiring with the other men in the dock to try to bamboozle the jury and to mislead my solicitors and me, all the accused, including my client, have pleaded guilty to all the charges.'

'That is certainly in their favour,' said the judge, 'but what has happened to the money?'

'I'll come to that in a moment, my lord.'

'I wish you'd come to it now.'

'I'd prefer,' said counsel, 'to present my case in my own way, my lord.'

'Well, of course I shall let you,' said the judge. 'But two and a half million pounds has been stolen. You ask me to give credit to this defendant for pleading guilty and I shall, but there isn't very much in that point, is there, if in fact the evidence of the prosecution was so overwhelming that the chances of their being acquitted were negligible. There is even less in it if, although they admit having had the money, they refuse to hand back what is left of it. I don't believe they have disposed of all that money in three weeks.'

'May I come to that in a moment, my lord?'

'Of course. But the longer you postpone your submission on this vital matter the more you will confirm my suspicion that none of the money will be forthcoming. Now let me make this plain. You cannot buy your way out of crime. Nevertheless, if a man who has stolen a very large sum of money hands back a substantial portion of it voluntarily, it is obviously a matter to be taken very seriously in his favour when it comes to sentence. No doubt you've all told this to your clients.'

'We have, my lord.'

'Of course,' went on the judge, 'if their idea is that it's worth while receiving a very long sentence if a very large sum of money will be awaiting them on their release, I can only warn them now while there is still time that the sentence is likely to be of such duration that certainly the older members of the gang may not be in a condition to enjoy the sort of life which the possession of a very large sum of money would enable them to enjoy today.'

'I quite see that, my lord,' said counsel.

'But do your clients?' asked the judge.

'My lord,' said counsel, 'I am fully instructed on that matter. Now if I may be allowed to return to my speech in mitigation. The second matter to which I wish to call your lordship's attention is that in this case there was no violence of any sort or kind.'

'There was no need for violence,' put in the judge. 'But do you say that if your client and his colleagues had been interrupted there would have been no violence?'

'They were not armed, my lord.'

'Only with spanners and similar instruments,' said the judge. 'Are you suggesting that such instruments would not have been used if they'd been interrupted? There was a vast sum of money at stake and your clients had spent a large sum of money in making preparations for their operation. It is difficult to believe that they would not have resisted if they'd been found out.'

'There is no evidence whatever that they would have done,' said counsel, 'and I hope your lordship is not going to sentence my client on the basis that this was robbery with violence. My client and his confederates went out of their way to ensure that, as far as possible, they were not disturbed during the robbery.'

'Doesn't every robber do that?' asked the judge. 'If you were going to steal something from someone else's safe, Mr Jenkins, surely you would go at a time when you hoped that the true owner wasn't there?'

'My lord,' said counsel, 'I have never considered such a possibility.'

'Well,' said the judge, 'consider it now, Mr Jenkins. Even the most wicked violent criminal wouldn't want to be disturbed if he could avoid it. Perhaps I should make it plain, Mr Jenkins, that I am not for the moment suggesting that you are a wicked, violent criminal.'

'Or a criminal at all, I hope,' said counsel.

'Certainly not,' said the judge. 'I took a bad example. I apologise.'

'Not at all, my lord,' said counsel. 'Of course my clients did not want to be disturbed. But I do want to draw your lordship's attention to the fact that they did not have any weapons with them with which to enable them to escape if they were disturbed. They didn't have a revolver or a cosh between them.'

'That may be so, Mr Jenkins,' said the judge, 'but they had spanners and other instruments, as I have already said. How am I to know for certain what would have happened? They weren't caught at the scene of the crime and they made a clean getaway. How can I tell what they were prepared to do if they had been disturbed?'

'Well, my lord, none of them attempted to evade arrest or to offer violence to the officers arresting them.'

'That's perfectly true,' said the judge.

'That being so, my lord, I don't see why your lordship shouldn't accept for the purpose of sentence that this was not a crime of violence.'

'Well,' said the judge, 'they blew open two safes. That's pretty violent, isn't it?'

'Only violence to property my lord, not to people. And, my lord, moreover, they are not charged with violence to people.'

'What would have happened if the night watchman had come along?' asked the judge. 'Would no violence of any kind have been offered to him? Would someone have just told him a few funny stories to distract his attention?'

'I think your lordship is forgetting,' said counsel, 'that the night watchman is in the dock.'

'Quite right, Mr Jenkins, I was. But suppose someone not in the conspiracy had come along?'

'I can only ask your lordship to accept my client's word. The word of a man who from first to last in this case has not told a single lie. I ask your lordship to accept that no violence would have been offered to anyone.'

'Well, Mr Jenkins, if it will help us to get to the real point of the case, that is, where the money is, any quicker, I will make that assumption in your client's favour.'

'Thank you, my lord. In those circumstances, my lord, I do suggest that there is a great deal to be said for my client in mitigation. No lies, no perjury, and no violence.'

'And no money,' said the judge.

'My lord, I fully realise that, if my client were able to offer substantial restitution, that would .go very much in his favour and I can assure your lordship that that has been made very clear to him.'

'I am sure it has, Mr Jenkins. Do you think it would help if I made it a bit clearer?'

'Your lordship has made it very clear indeed.'

'Would you like to take fresh instructions, Mr Jenkins?' asked the judge. 'Just in case your client thinks that he is going to be sent away for a few years and then come out to enjoy the fruits of the robbery, let me make it quite plain that, subject to anything further you may say, he is going away for many many years. There is a further consideration I should mention. By the time he comes out the value of money may have so dropped that the amount which he has hidden in the earth or put away somewhere may be of only trifling value. Let him think of that, Mr Jenkins.'

'All those considerations have been pointed out to the accused, my lord.'

'And they still refuse to say where any of the money is?'

'They don't refuse, my lord, they simply don't say.'

'You say they don't refuse,' said the judge. 'Well, you are representing Mr Gladstone and I ask you now, Mr Jenkins. Where is the money? Are you going to tell me or not?'

'My lord,' said counsel, 'if I knew where the money was I should have informed the proper authority.'

'But you are acting for Mr Gladstone,' said the judge. 'Naturally I am not asking you on your own behalf. I am asking you on Mr Gladstone's behalf to tell me where the money is or such portion of it as is left.' The judge paused and waited for an answer. There was none. 'Well, Mr Jenkins,' he went on, 'if your silence isn't a refusal I don't know what refusal is. Now don't let's waste any more time about this. Have you anything more to say in mitigation that does not relate to the whereabouts of the money?'

'No, my lord,' said counsel.

'Very well, then, you said you were coming to the money later and now that time has come. Are you going to tell the Court where any of it is?'

'I'm afraid I'm unable to do that, my lord. My client has given me no instructions on the subject.'

'And I assume from that,' said the judge, 'that, even if I adjourned the case, you would still have no instructions on the subject.'

'That is so, my lord.'

'Very well then. I'll hear what's to be said on behalf of the other accused.'

Several speeches were then made by counsel, all much to the same effect as that of counsel for Mr Gladstone. The judge passed sentence and then adjourned for the day. The case had not taken as long as had been expected owing to the prisoners' pleas of guilty. Accordingly, the judge arrived at his club not long after lunch.

'Hullo, Charles,' said a member, David Puddefoot, 'I didn't expect to see you here. I thought you were trying the bank robbery case.'

'Quite right.'

'But wasn't it going to take weeks? Weren't there twelve prisoners all defended by counsel?'

'That's right.'

'And Gladstone was the ringleader?'

'Right again.'

'One thing I'd like to know,' said Puddefoot, 'did they all have legal aid?'

'They did,' said the judge.

'But that's outrageous. Why should I pay for the defence of people who've got away with over two million pounds? They could afford to pay for counsel themselves.'

'But suppose they said they hadn't got away with the money and hadn't any of their own?'

'That's all very well, but they're obviously guilty.'

'Then why bother to try them? If a man says he's not guilty he's got to be tried and tried fairly.'

'I don't mind his being tried,' said Puddefoot, 'but I don't see why I should pay for it. They get legal aid by saying they're not guilty and then what happens when they're convicted?'

'Suppose they were refused legal aid and were then acquitted? As a matter of fact it's a good thing in this case that they did have legal aid. Counsel talked some sense into them and they all pleaded guilty.'

'Good gracious,' said Puddefoot, 'so they admit they've got the money.'

'They admitted they'd taken the money but not that they've still got it.'

'But they can't have got rid of two and a half million pounds in three weeks before they were arrested. I must say I give the police full marks for catching them within a month.'

'I quite agree.'

'Well, where's the money?'

'You may well ask.'

'I do.'

'Well, we did too,' said the judge, 'but with no effect. I did my best to coax them but none of them would tell me.'

'Well, how much did you give Gladstone?'

'How much would you have given him?'

'There's too much of this sort of thing going on. Organised crime is taking place on a very big scale and when they're caught it must be shown to them that it doesn't pay. Let me think, Yes, I think I'd have given him twenty-five years. D'you think that's too much?'

'Not a day too long. That's what I gave him.'

'Well, I suppose he'll come out long before that. What's the good of your giving him twenty-five years if the Home Secretary lets him out after five.'

'Oh, he won't do that.'

'Well, when will he come out?'

'He gets a third remission for good conduct, which means that, if he gets no further remission and the Parole Board do nothing about him, he would come out after sixteen years.'

'From what I read, nobody seems to stay as long as that even for murder.'

'That's perfectly true. I expect he'll be there for about ten.'

At that moment a club servant came up to the judge. 'Excuse me, Sir Charles. There's a police officer wants to see you,' he said.

'A police officer?' queried the judge. 'I put my car on a meter. At least I'm sure I did. Which means I'm not quite sure. Perhaps I made a mistake and put it on the wrong side.'

'I don't think it's that, sir,' said the club servant. 'It's an inspector.'

'Forgive me, David,' said the judge, 'I'll be back.'

'I hope so,' said Puddefoot. 'Don't make a statement without being cautioned.'

The judge went to the entrance hall where a detective inspector was waiting.

'I'm Detective Inspector Holmes, sir,' he said, 'I'm extremely sorry to trouble you at your club, but I thought you ought to know something.'

'Oh?' said the judge. 'What is it?'

'The prisoner Gladstone has escaped.'

'Escaped?' said the judge. 'Already?'

'Yes, my lord.'

'Well, I'm not surprised he didn't want to say where the money was. When did it happen?'

'On the way back from the court, my lord,' said the inspector. 'Two fire engines, sounding their sirens, appeared. One of them blocked the road in front of the car in which Gladstone was and the other rammed the car and overturned it. The firemen then helped the occupants out and took away Gladstone and the detective to whom he was handcuffed in another car which was standing by. They weren't, of course, firemen at all and the two fire engines had been stolen.'

'Stolen?' said the judge. 'How did they manage that?'

'It was comparatively simple,' said the inspector. 'There was a false alarm and when the two engines had reached the place the firemen were overpowered by about a dozen men, trussed up and put into a waiting van. Some of the men then made off with the fire engines. We've got the number of the car in which Gladstone was taken off, but I'm afraid that won't be much help because they will have changed it in a few minutes and left it abandoned somewhere. A cordon has been put round the area and let's hope he gets caught in it, but he may not try to get through it. Very likely he will go to a good hotel.'

'But won't he be recognized?' asked the judge. 'His picture has been in the papers.'

'He may be,' said the inspector, 'but on the whole people don't see what they don't expect to see. Very likely he'll bandage up one eye and wear dark glasses or something of that sort. Naturally hotel receptionists don't like calling the police to investigate their customers.'

'Naturally,' said the judge, 'but surely after the hue and cry is raised they'll think about possible candidates who have just come to their hotels.'

'They'll try,' said the inspector, 'but probably he won't book a room himself. One of his confederates whose picture has not appeared will go to the reception desk while he'll sit quietly in the lounge. Very likely he'll stay there for a couple of months until he's grown a beard and a moustache.'

'Won't anybody give him away?'

'It's very unlikely,' said the inspector, 'with all that money around. They can get more out of him than they will out of us. He's probably taken a suite at the Ritz or something of that kind.'

'How long does it take to grow a decent size beard and moustache?'

'Well, I'm not an expert,' said the inspector, 'but I gather it can be done in about five or six weeks. Enough to avoid immediate recognition anyway.'

'Meantime,' said the judge, 'he has to stay in his room. Won't that make some of the hotel staff suspicious?'

'But they won't know,' said the inspector. 'He's probably got a woman with him and certainly another man. Unless the chambermaid and the floor waiter and the porter and the receptionist and the housekeeper all compare notes they won't know that none of them have seen him. And in a big hotel why should they bother? And, as I said, hotels don't like suspecting their guests. The chances are ten to one or more that anybody whom they do suspect is a perfectly inoffensive person. But possibly he won't go to an hotel, and will use some confederate's flat instead. He can stay there as long as he likes without anybody being any wiser. They can't keep a cordon round the area indefinitely. And after eight or nine weeks or so, with a beard and a moustache and probably a wig, he goes anywhere he likes. Probably he'll get a forged passport.'

'He'll have to be photographed for that,' said the judge.

'Of course,' said the inspector, 'but he'll be photographed with his new face and his new name will be Arnold Macintosh of 25 Playfair Buildings. Occupation managing director or the like. We'll get him again, my lord, but it may take years.'

'Well, thank you very much, Inspector,' said the judge, and went back to his friend and told him what had happened.

'Good God!' said Puddefoot. 'What's the good of catching them if you can't keep them? All the same I shouldn't like to be in Mr Gladstone's shoes now. I often think about these people who've escaped from prison. They can never know when they're suddenly going to be identified and a hand put on their shoulder. However much time goes by they are never safe. It must be a horrible feeling.'

'Quite right, David,' said the judge. 'And the strain on their wives and girlfriends, when they know what the position is, must be almost as bad or worse. Whenever the telephone rings, whenever there's a knock at the door, whenever a stranger asks for a light or to know the way or something of that sort they must wonder if he is a policeman or an informer. Whenever they go out in public, are they recognised by someone? The strain on the nerves must be terrible. And even after some years when you hope you've outwitted everybody there's always the possibility that you haven't. Always the possibility that someone's going to give you away. Always the possibility that by one of those horrible coincidences that turn up when you least want them, you're going to be found out and then it will certainly be the end. They'll make quite sure that you don't escape again.'

'Well, I hope Mr Gladstone doesn't have too much time to worry about the possibility of recapture.'

'The next six weeks are the most important, it seems to me,' said the judge. 'The inspector told me that's about the time it will take him to grow a moustache and beard. At least they've got his fingerprints and if they do find him they can prove that he's the man.'

'Are fingerprints an absolute certainty?'

'To all intents and purposes. I believe there was a case many years ago when a mistake was made, but for practical purposes fingerprints are foolproof.'

'I wonder what he'll do when he comes out of hiding?'

'Oh, go abroad. The inspector says it's easy for him to get a forged passport. The inspector seemed confident that they'd catch him in the end. They usually do, but not always. They haven't caught Biggs yet, though apparently they came pretty near to it.'

'Doesn't it make you feel rather frustrated?'

'Not really,' said the judge.

'But you take the trouble to try a man and take the trouble to give him twenty-five years and off he goes rejoicing and cocking a snook at you. You've just been wasting your time.'

'That's unavoidable. It's worse for the police and they must be furious. They are responsible for keeping him in custody. I'm not.'

'But you said twenty-five years and as far as I can see, he didn't serve more than twenty-five minutes.'

'He probably will, and, as you said, every minute until he is caught he'll have hanging over him the dread that the fatal day may yet come. No, I wouldn't be in his shoes.'

'You'd prefer to be serving twenty-five years, would you?'

'That's a good point,' said the judge. 'Which is the worse? Fear or despair?'

'Despair any day. At least there's some excitement in fear.'

CHAPTER THREE

Dinner Party

On the morning after Gladstone escaped Mrs Winchcombe heard about it on the seven o'clock news. She immediately moved into action.

'Wake up, Henry,' she said to her husband. As he didn't respond she shook him by the shoulders. 'Wake up,' she said, 'there's a lot to be done.'

'Leave me alone,' said Henry sleepily. It was the only time in the day when he did not respond immediately to his wife's voice.

'Henry,' she said, 'behave yourself. You're not in your dreams with your Arabian slave girl now.'

'What Arabian?' said Henry sleepily.

'All right,' said Mrs Winchcombe, 'you've asked for it,' and she pulled off the bedclothes. 'Any more nonsense and you shall have a glass of cold water over you.'

'I'm sorry, dear,' said Henry. 'Was there something?'

'I've just heard the news,' said his wife, 'and we've got a dinner party tonight.'

'Did they mention it then?' said Henry.

'Don't try to be funny. It's too early in the morning for that.'

'It's too early in the morning full stop,' said Henry. He was instinctively aware that this was the only time of the day when he could say what he thought and he was enjoying the pleasant experience for as long as possible.

'Now listen to me,' said Mrs Winchcombe. 'We've got a dinner party tonight and Gladstone the bank robber has escaped.'

'We hadn't invited him, had we?' said Henry.

'Give me patience,' said Mrs Winchcombe.

'Amen,' said her husband.

Mrs Winchcombe was equally aware that the only time when her husband was a little difficult was early in the morning, particularly if he was disturbed from his sleep. On this occasion he'd been woken up in the middle of a very pleasant waking dream and he would very much have liked to have known what had happened. But as the dream had faded completely from his memory almost as soon as he woke up it was impossible even to invent an end of the adventure. Most annoying.

'Well, had we?' he said, 'but I suppose we couldn't have because they wouldn't have let him out on bail just to dine with us. No one could say our dinner parties are like a funeral.'

'No,' said Mrs Winchcombe, 'we had not asked Gladstone to join us. Nor – nor – ' she emphasised the 'nor' ' – nor have we asked the judge.'

'Oh, we can ask him next time,' said Henry.

'Has it not yet entered your head,' said Mrs Winchcombe, 'that the person above all who ought to talk to us tonight is the judge?'

Mrs Winchcombe always tried to arrange her dinner parties so that if any particular event had occurred within two or three weeks, there was someone present to be able to talk on the subject. An expert. If a woman had quins, she wanted a doctor. If a bridge had collapsed, an engineer. If a block of flats had fallen down, an architect and so on. The theft of two and a half million pounds, although not as dramatic as it would have been ten years previously, was certainly of a sensational order, the pleas of guilty by all the accused were a little unusual and you certainly did not hear of sentences of twenty-five years' imprisonment every other day of the week. When you add to that the immediate escape of the main culprit, it was plain that this story would be the chief topic of conversation at dinner. And Hamlet had not been asked.

'You must ring him up immediately after breakfast,' she said, 'and explain what has happened.'

'But he'll read that in the paper,' said Henry.

'I mean,' said Mrs Winchcombe, 'explain that you thought I'd asked them and I'd thought you'd asked them. Apologise profusely and ask if there's any possibility that they can still come.'

'You'd do it better than me,' said Henry, and very boldly added, 'you're a better liar.'

Mrs Winchcombe was surprised, but contented herself with saying: 'Have your bath and get dressed.' Then she decided that Henry was probably right and that she would do it better than he would. So at half past nine precisely she went to the telephone and dialled the number of the judge. The judge's wife answered.

'I do apologise for ringing so early in the morning,' said Mrs Winchcombe, 'but a terrible thing has happened.'

'Isn't it?' said Mrs Ward. 'On the same day that he was sentenced. I can't think what the police were doing.'

'Actually,' said Mrs Winchcombe, 'I wasn't ringing up about that.'

'What a pity,' said Mrs Ward. 'Bertie's furious about it.'

'Actually,' said Mrs Winchcombe, 'it was about you and Bertie.'

'Really? What have we done then?'

'It's what *we haven't done*,' said Mrs Winchcombe, 'but what we hope you will do.'

'How clearly you put things,' said Mrs Ward. 'Just like Bertie.'

'The truth is,' said Mrs Winchcombe, 'that we're having a few friends here for dinner tonight.'

'I do hope it keeps fine for you, then you'll be able to have drinks out of doors.'

'Thank you,' said Mrs Winchcombe. 'But what I really wanted to say was this. Quite honestly I thought you were coming.'

'What a shame you never asked us.'

'To be quite truthful,' said Mrs Winchcombe, 'I thought we had.'

'Did we accept then?'

'It's all a misunderstanding,' said Mrs Winchcombe.

'I suppose Henry asked Bertie and Bertie forgot to tell me.'

'That's very nearly it,' said Mrs Winchcombe. 'What actually happened was this. I was going to write and ask you and then Henry said that he'd be seeing Bertie and he'd do it for me and then he forgot. Well, I don't mean that exactly. The truth of the matter is that he thought I was telephoning you and I thought he was telephoning Bertie.'

'And then,' said Mrs Ward, 'you forgot to ask each other what the answer was. I do sympathise. I'm always doing the same sort of thing myself.'

'How understanding you are,' said Mrs Winchcombe.

'How nice of you to say so,' said Mrs Ward. 'Yes, I understand perfectly. You want Bertie to come along and talk about the Gladstone case. As a matter of fact, before he left for court this morning I warned him this would probably happen.'

'How very fortunate,' said Mrs Winchcombe. 'And can you both possibly come?'

'We shall be delighted.'

'I'm so glad,' said Mrs Winchcombe, and made a mental note that never in any circumstances in the future, unless it were absolutely essential, would she invite Mrs Ward to her house again. From time to time Mrs Winchcombe made mental notes of this kind but as nobody else knew about them, she was at liberty to disregard them whenever she felt inclined.

The dinner party was a huge success. Mrs Winchcombe herself introduced the subject.

'Tell me, Bertie, d'you think twenty-five years was too much?'

'Gladstone thought so apparently,' said the judge.

'That's a new one on me,' put in the commander. 'Should you only give the prisoner a sentence which he's prepared to serve? If you give him too much he'll escape. Is that it?'

'It's an idea,' said the judge. 'But, on the whole, I think the present method of sentencing is all wrong. Dangerous men like Gladstone should be shut up for life. Most of the non-dangerous prisoners shouldn't be in prison at all. Dr Johnson is supposed to have said that half the people in prison shouldn't be there and that half should never come out. I think there's a good deal to be said for that. Personally, I think that a dangerous man should be shut up tight in decent conditions and never released until a panel like the Committee at Broadmoor certifies that it's safe to release him.'

'You keep on saying "he",' said Mrs Winchcombe. 'What about the women? Where do we come in?'

'I'm glad to say you don't really,' said the judge. 'There are so few of you that you don't create any problem. Of the people at present in prison, do you know that only about one in forty is a woman?'

'But why did they let Gladstone get away?' said the commander's wife.

'I don't know that they let him,' said the judge. 'There are, of course, a few corrupt policemen but not many, and it is difficult to believe that the firemen were bribed as well. It was quite a brilliant idea, as a matter of fact. None of the policemen suspected that the two fire engines weren't going lawfully about their business and even when the collision occurred they must have thought it was just owing to the way in which the engines were being driven. Before they had time to realise their mistake Gladstone was away. If only these people would use their ingenuity for lawful purposes they could be very useful members of the community.'

'What was Gladstone?' asked the commander.

'According to the police,' said the judge, 'he was just an educated criminal.'

'Why does a man like that take to crime?' asked Mrs Winchcombe.

'Less work and bigger prizes, I suppose,' said the judge.

'Tremendous risks,' put in the commander.

'For some men,' said the judge, 'that makes it all the more exciting. I have known people during the war who enjoyed danger. Not many, I grant you, and I certainly wasn't one of them. Most climbers, I suppose, must enjoy the risk as well as the sense of achievement.'

'You have so much power, Bertie,' said Mrs Winchcombe. 'What does it feel like when you send a man to prison for all those years?'

'Well, I've never done it,' said the judge. 'I'm only a circuit judge and don't try the most serious cases. The most I've ever given a man is ten years.'

'That's enough, in all conscience,' said the commander, 'isn't it? Just think of the power it implies. You and your fellow judges alone in the community have the power to deprive a man of his freedom for ten whole years. Indeed, as you say, some of you can deprive him for longer. But just think. Ten years being ordered about. Ten years of probably sharing accommodation with somebody you can't stand. Ten years of bad food, cold and not very sanitary conditions, yes ten years of smell, so I've read. That's all right for people who have been brought up in it. It's not so bad for regular criminals, people who sleep rough when they are out of prison and to whom the inside of a prison may indeed be a relief after the greater cold and hunger outside. But apparently this man has never been to prison before. He's a chap like you and me.'

'He certainly has a higher standard than me,' said the judge, 'if what the police say is true. They say he's well educated. And I'm certainly not well educated.'

'Oh come, judge,' said Mrs Winchcombe, 'don't be so modest. We all know you are.'

'Oh no, Hester, I'm not. Granted I'm supposed to be. I've had all the opportunities but did I take them? Certainly not. Very few of us do. I know a certain amount about the law because I have to. I've had to earn my living at it. I know a little about monumental brasses. I've read a certain amount. I've seen a few pictures and I've listened to a little music. But educated! Good gracious me, no. Ask me some fairly simple questions about Shakespeare. Probably the greatest poet in the world. And one of our most important possessions. Ask me a simple question about him. The chances are I shall not be able to answer. Or if you ask me something about political economy or ecology or astronomy.'

'Or croquet?' put in the commander.

'Well, yes,' conceded the judge, 'I know a little about croquet but nobody could say I am an expert any more than you are. What does the average well-educated man know? Precious little. The best I can do is to hold my own among those who are educated a little worse than I am.'

'Meaning us, I suppose,' said Mrs Winchcombe.

'I wouldn't for a moment say you are less educated than I am,' said the judge. 'You, for example, are an expert on farming. You probably have as much knowledge as I have of the Victorian classics, Bach and Beethoven, Manet and Monet, and possibly of the modern composers and artists as well. I expect your knowledge of political economy is better than mine too, because you are partially concerned with it.'

'And what about me?' said the commander. 'Do you consider me better or less educated than you are?'

'I shouldn't think there's much in it,' said the judge. 'You know a lot about quarterdecks, a good deal about the sea and a lot about man management. Possibly my knowledge of literature and music exceeds yours, but I would be very hesitant to say that it did.'

'I wonder what music Mr Gladstone likes best,' said Mrs Winchcombe.

'I wonder how long he'll be able to hear it for,' said the judge 'They'll catch up with him in the end.'

'D'you feel sure of it?' said Mrs Winchcombe.

'They nearly always do,' said the judge, 'even though it takes them a year or two or even several years. They'll get him in the end. Probably some girl will give him away.'

'He's sure to go abroad, I suppose,' said the commander.

'Probably,' said the judge. 'Certainly to begin with. He might come back to England and settle down somewhere in the country and establish a new identity for himself. He may well have some plastic surgery done abroad, so that his face won't be recognisable even if he doesn't grow a moustache and a beard. Then, if he hasn't run through all his money, he might take a house in some country spot like this, for example, and merge into the neighbourhood. Why should anyone suspect him? That's the trouble with 'wanted' men. At first too many people see them and the police are inundated with information which lands them in dozens of wild goose chases. And later on nobody sees them.'

'What would you do,' said Mrs Winchcombe, 'if he settled down here? If he turned out to be a really nice chap and got on well with all of us. What would you do if you suddenly discovered that he was the wanted man?'

'Go to the police of course,' said the judge.

'Even if he'd become a great friend of yours?' said the commander's wife.

'That would depend upon how deep the friendship was,' said the judge.

'Supposing,' said the commander's wife, 'you had a small child and he'd saved its life. Would that make any difference?'

The judge thought for a moment. 'Yes,' he said, 'I suppose it might be that I should consider my obligation to the man greater than my obligation to the community. It's one of the decisions people have to take from time to time, and as the ordinary human being that I am, I can't pretend that I should rise above natural human failings. But this kind of thing is always happening.'

'I didn't know that bank robbers escaped so often,' said Mrs Winchcombe.

'I didn't mean that,' said the judge. 'I mean the sort of case where a man on the run is befriended by his wife. Would anyone here blame her? I certainly shouldn't and if I had a woman charged with aiding and abetting the escape of her husband or, indeed, her lover or son or daughter I very much doubt whether I should impose a sentence of imprisonment. The law has to make it a crime to shield the criminal, whatever your relationship with that criminal may be, whatever your duty to that criminal may be. But that's because society has to have these fixed rules. That doesn't necessarily mean that in every case where a person breaks the law he is breaking his moral duty. In other words, he may be morally right though legally wrong. I wonder what other people think about this? Henry, you haven't said very much so far. If your wife came back one day and told you that she'd knocked somebody down and had panicked and run off, would you turn her over to the police?'

'*Would* you?' said Mrs Winchcombe.

'Well, I suppose – ' began her husband hesitantly. 'I should want to know what had happened to the injured person.'

'Whatever I did,' said Mrs Winchcombe, 'I would not have left an injured person unattended on the road.'

'All right,' said the judge, 'let's assume there was no personal injury. Let's assume it was a few days before your car insurance was to be renewed and you had made no claims during the year. Let's assume she bashed into an immaculate Rolls-Royce which was standing stationary in the road and that then she panicked and made off home before anybody had time to find out who'd done it. If you were a mechanic, Henry, would you help to repair her car so that there would be no mark on it to give away what had happened as soon as somebody started making enquiries?'

Before he could reply Mrs Winchcombe said: 'Of course I would never dream of doing such a thing, but, just to let the judge have his example, suppose I did? Well, it would be my responsibility and I hope my husband would do what I said. If I were caught I would carry the can but it would be up to him to help me. He married me for better or worse. What d'you say, vicar?'

'Well, this certainly would have been worse,' said the vicar, 'but I personally have strong views on the subject. I think that a husband and wife should stand by each other in all circumstances.'

'Even in the case of danger to the country?' asked the judge. 'Even if one of them turned out to be a spy?'

'All the more so,' said the vicar. 'Naturally to comply with what I consider to be a spouse's first moral duty might land the one who helped in prison if the truth were found out. That doesn't alter the moral duty in cases where a husband or wife might have to give information against the other unless the criminal conduct might affect the children.'

'Well,' said the judge, 'indirectly it might affect the children if a nuclear secret were sold to an enemy. It might result in the children being blown up.'

'That,' said the vicar, 'is what I think you lawyers call "too remote". But what about friends?' he went on.

'What are friends?' said the judge. 'You start by being an acquaintance and then the acquaintanceship ripens into friendship. How deep must that friendship be to require you to break the law? No doubt the vicar's about to say that greater love hath no man than this, that a man shall lay down his life for his friends. But that doesn't solve the question. Who are his friends for this purpose? How many of us have a dozen friends to whom we could safely admit that we had committed a very grave crime, such as murder. I was thinking about that the other day and I came to the conclusion that, though in one sense I have many friends, there are at the most half a dozen to whom I could make such an admission. It would not be fair to the others to burden them with the responsibility.'

'What about the six?' asked the vicar. 'Would they be right not to give you away?'

'I think so,' said the judge. 'Just as I think I should be right not to give them away. Of course anyone in a public position like me would have to resign if he did such a thing.'

'In other words,' said the vicar, 'you consider that a deep friendship is as sacred as a family relationship?'

'I think that's a fair way of putting it,' said the judge, 'but we still don't know what Henry would do if his wife came home with a damaged car and told him that she'd run into this immaculate Rolls-Royce. First of all, would you try to persuade your wife to go and inform the police?'

'Certainly,' said Henry.

'And when that failed?' said Mrs Winchcombe enquiringly.

'Well,' said Henry, after a pause, but with surprising eloquence, 'I've been on her side for over twenty years and I should remain so.'

To everyone's surprise the hardheaded Mrs Winchcombe gulped and very nearly burst into tears.

'Would you mind passing me the butter?' said Henry.

'So I suppose the answer is,' said the judge, 'that if Mr Granger, formerly Gladstone, came here and lived with us for, say, ten years, so that there was ample time for a deep friendship to develop between him and any one or more of us, then such a friend would not give him away but anyone less well acquainted with him would feel bound to do so.'

'Let's hope it happens,' said the commander. 'It would bring some excitement into the village.'

'I don't think you'd find it exciting at all,' said the judge. 'If the chap came here and we found out about him within a short time then it would, of course, be exciting, and there would be no problem for us. We'd simply hand him over to the police. But if he were here for many years and had become really part of us, the problem which each one of us would have to face would not be in the least exciting. Depressing rather.'

'Well, I think that's enough of that,' said Mrs Winchcombe. 'What do you think of the claret, judge? You know something about claret, I believe?'

'Nothing like as much as Henry,' said the judge, 'but I did learn something about it at a very early age. When I joined Gray's Inn as a student they gave us Château-Lafite 1899.'

'Good God!' said Henry.

'Henry!' said Mrs Winchcombe.

'That's all right, Hester,' said the vicar. 'I heard worse than that when I was in the Army.'

'You are not in the Army now, Harvey,' said Mrs Winchcombe. 'Nor is Henry.'

'But those days are past,' said the judge. 'The cellar was bombed during the war and from what I hear, the present students get something more like plonk than Château-Lafite '99, but it gave me a taste for the wine.'

'What would you say this is?' asked Henry.

'I should say it was a '53,' said the judge.

'Quite right,' said Mr Winchcombe. 'Can you carry it any further? You ought to be able to.'

'Now you've told him, Henry,' said Mrs Winchcombe.

'It's a Lafite, is it?' said the judge. 'I couldn't have guessed, but it's quite delicious.'

'A fitting reward, don't you think?' said the judge's wife.

'Reward?' queried the judge.

'Your wife means,' said Mrs Winchcombe, 'that you deserved something of the sort for holding forth so well.'

'That means,' said the judge, 'that I've been talking too much. I don't apologise. You all know that I do and I suppose you wouldn't ask me if you didn't like it.'

'The truth of the matter is,' said Mrs Winchcombe, who under the influence of the claret had decided to make a frontal attack on the judge's wife, 'the truth of the matter is that we invited you here to talk about the bank robber. If he'd escaped three weeks ago you'd have been invited with all the others. But as it was only last night, you weren't invited until this morning. Naturally I didn't like to say that when I invited you, because your wife might have taken offence and have refused to come. Now you both know the truth.'

'I knew it from the start,' said the judge's wife.

'I did wonder myself,' said the judge, 'but, so long as I'm free, I don't mind when I'm given an attractive invitation. It's an advantage really to be asked late because if one doesn't want to go, one can refuse without giving offence.'

'I wonder if we might revert to the bank robbery for the moment,' said the vicar. 'If you'd been the judge how much would you have taken off if one of the men had told you where the money was? In other words, if he'd let down all his colleagues and given the game away.'

'Oh, a lot,' said the judge. 'I'm afraid we don't want to encourage honour among thieves. On the contrary. Indeed there have been cases where they've let a man off altogether for giving his friends away. I'm referring to cases where it's generally known as "turning Queen's evidence". There isn't such a thing technically today but it has the same effect. If one of the gang says he will give evidence against all the others and the police case is not complete without such evidence they often don't prosecute him at all.'

'It hasn't a very nice smell about it,' said the commander.

'Of course it hasn't,' said the judge, 'but crime altogether hasn't a very nice smell about it. One has to think of the public as a whole and of the injured party and, even if the injured party's a bank, the return of a million pounds or even several hundred thousand can be quite useful to a bank. But I must say I can't help admiring the way in which these chaps stand together. Though I suppose in most cases it's simply due to fear. I wouldn't like to underwrite the life of a man who informed against twenty bank robbers. If he stayed in the country, he'd pretty well need police protection for the rest of his days.'

'As we've gone back to crime,' said Mrs Winchcombe, 'what's your answer, judge, to the mounting wave of violence and vandalism?'

'We need more police,' said the judge. 'Double the numbers and a higher standard of intelligence. Sir Robert Peel's Force has lasted getting on for a hundred and fifty years, but in my view it needs a complete overhaul. On the whole the police are very good fellows, there is very little corruption among them and most of them are striving to do a very difficult job as well as they can. But unfortunately quite a number of them haven't a high enough standard of intelligence. So if you ask me what I would do if I were in authority, the answer's quite simple. I should double the pay and raise the standard of entry. The Police Force would compete with the other Services and with the professions and other occupations for young men and women of good physique and a reasonably high standard of intelligence for entrants. It's much better to prevent crime than to award astronomic sentences as a deterrent. The best deterrent against crime is the certainty of conviction. It's well known that if you get a large number of police in any particular area the rate of crime drops immediately, but if you cried for help in a London street today on how many occasions would it be heard by a policeman? Very few. I want to see the policeman on the beat again.'

'But,' said the commander, 'if he's going to be paid double what he's being paid now, wouldn't he be overpaid? I mean, wouldn't the ordinary uniformed policeman be getting too much?'

'I don't think so,' said the judge. 'In the first place, as I said, you've got to encourage a high standard of entrant. In the second place, the policeman on the beat performs a very useful function indeed and he ought to be well paid. It has been admitted that the pay of the police is a special case and, if the Government really want to protect the country from the wave of violence and vandalism from which we are now suffering, I think it's the main way of doing it. We sometimes get the weather from the United States. Let's hope, that we don't inherit their crime rate in the same way. The situation in the streets of New York is quite intolerable. It is not safe for women to walk after dark and even men have to be extremely careful by day and by night. I'm told that you are advised always to carry some money on you lest you be attacked by a couple of drug fiends who want money with which to buy drugs. If they find you've got nothing on you, they may stick a knife into you because they are so frantic. This isn't the case in England yet, but the time to ward off the possibility is now – before it's happened.'

'I quite agree,' said the commander. 'The same sort of thing happened in 1938 when the Government took wholly insufficient steps to rearm and in consequence we were faced with a war in 1939. I can't for the life of me think why somebody doesn't do something about it.'

'Well, I *can* think why they don't do anything about it,' said the judge. 'It certainly wouldn't be easy because, if you seek to convert the Police Force into a very highly paid Force, the Army, the Navy and the Air Force might start to complain and the trades unions certainly would. They would say the differential had gone all wrong. The Government's got so much on its plate it doesn't want trouble. But the answer to both arguments in my view is that, unless they do face that situation now, they may have to face a far worse situation when in fact it's too late. This claret really is delicious. And the other thing I'd do, as I said, is to shut up dangerous men for ever.'

'If you feel so strongly about it,' said Mrs Winchcombe, 'why don't *you* do something about it?'

'I can't,' said the judge, 'because sitting judges don't as a matter of tradition take part in politics. And this is politics. It is dealing with the running of the country. My only job is to try cases. It is perfectly true that we can occasionally in a judgment call attention to the fact that something seems to require reform, but we can't go stumping up and down the country trying to promote this or that policy. We can call attention to the shortage of police, but we can't go on television, for example, and try to convince the public of the necessity of persuading the Government to reorganize the Police Force. And that's what's required. The Government will very rarely move unless it sees votes in the transaction. What some public-spirited individual has got to do is to convince the public of the necessity of reforming the Police Force on the lines that I've mentioned and to put pressure on the Government to get something done about it.'

41

'Then why don't you retire and do it?' said the commander.

'For several reasons,' said the judge. 'First of all I prefer from my own selfish point of view to remain a judge and to be paid the salary of a judge and do the work of a judge. Secondly, I probably wouldn't be any good at it. Thirdly, I certainly haven't at the moment any influence with the public at all. Except in his own area the ordinary Circuit judge isn't known to the public.'

'When will you be retiring?' said Mrs Winchcombe.

'Oh not for some years. I've got at least ten years to go and possibly longer,' said the judge. 'Anyway I'm not an agitator. I'm not a politician. I don't suppose I'm much of a judge but that's what I think I can do best and I propose to stick to it. But any of you, if you feel strongly enough about it, can badger your local Member of Parliament to try and get him to do something. But it's an uphill job. The truth of the matter is that in modern times there is so much for politicians to do that they don't welcome anything additional. They will find all sorts of excuses for not doing it. It's only really when something big happens that you get some kind of action. The same applies to the permanent Civil Service. They don't want change because they've got quite enough to do without it. The best example I know in recent years of change being compelled by public opinion was in the Ministry of Transport. The Ministry, which really means the civil servants, had been resisting for a long time the idea of putting barriers between the two lanes on motorways, and successive Ministers of Transport had accepted the advice given to them by the civil servants. It was only after there'd been several head-on collisions in quick succession, resulting in heavy loss of life, that public opinion compelled the Ministry of Transport to go into reverse and to agree to put up the barriers. Up till then, because of the expense, they had convinced themselves that the arguments for not putting up barriers were stronger than the arguments for putting them up, when in my view any fool could have seen that it was the other way round.'

CHAPTER FOUR

The Views of Mary Buckland

On the day after the dinner party the vicar called on the local store and post office which was run by Mr and Mrs Buckland. Mr Buckland had married late in life and his very attractive wife was twenty-five years younger than he was. They were a very happy couple and they enjoyed running the business with reasonable inefficiency.

'Morning, vicar,' said Mr Buckland, 'did you like our carrots?'

'What carrots?' said the vicar.

'Yes,' said Mr Buckland, 'our carrots. The gardener must be off or something at Broadway House. We got a sudden urgent order for half a dozen tins of young carrots.'

'I'd have sworn they weren't tinned.'

'Here you are then, vicar,' said Mrs Buckland, 'ten new pence a tin.'

'I shall have to wait till after Easter for that,' said the vicar. 'I can't afford these luxuries. They certainly were very nice.'

'And what about the smoked salmon?' said Mrs Buckland.

'It wasn't yours too?' said the vicar.

'No, it wasn't, as a matter of fact, but the man from Brinton left it here and we sent it up with the carrots.'

'Perhaps you know what we talked about as well as what we ate,' said the vicar.

'Well, that's easy,' said Mr Buckland. 'Mrs Ward rang up and cancelled her sausages, so I knew that the judge and she were going at the last moment. Of course she wanted him to talk about the bank robber.'

'Your intelligence service,' said the vicar, 'is very efficient. Can one subscribe to it?'

'It's free to every customer,' said Mr Buckland.

'I wonder where he's gone?' said Mrs Buckland. 'I wish he'd come here. We've got a spare room.'

'You'd give him shelter, would you?' asked the vicar.

'If I were away,' said Mr Buckland, 'she would. She's too soft-hearted. We don't get many tramps or gipsies these days, thank heaven. If we did, she'd give away the whole of our stock.'

'I wish everyone were like Mrs Buckland,' said the vicar.

'Well, their husbands would be out of business,' said Mr Buckland, 'if they were. But, seriously, would you let your wife conceal an escaped criminal?'

'Certainly not!' said the vicar.

'There's no romance in life today,' said Mrs Buckland.

'There's no romance in bank robbers,' said the vicar. 'Nor was there in the old days of highwaymen. The only romantic part of a highwayman was his horse. Otherwise they were just as much thugs and cut-throats as the thugs and cut-throats of today.'

'But didn't they raise their hats and bow and kiss the ladies' hands when they held up a coach?'

'I've no doubt that all depended on what they wanted,' said the vicar. 'I've had a certain amount of experience of criminals. I was a prison chaplain for a time. I was also an army chaplain and there were several criminals in my unit.'

'What did you think of them?' asked Mrs Buckland.

'Lots of the chaps in prison were very nice. They have to be. They vary, of course, like everyone else. Except in some extreme pathological cases you really wouldn't know them from an ordinary law-abiding chap. Most of them are very pleasant to talk to, but that's when they are in custody and a good number I shouldn't like to meet on a dark night. Whether it's their fault or not, heaven knows, but one doesn't have time to consider that on a dark night. And a dozen free range eggs, please. And might I ask a question about the eggs?'

'Of course,' said Mrs Buckland.

'I know you've got your own hens and they're running about cheerfully but you don't seem to have enough to supply all the free range eggs that people round there buy from you.'

'No, we haven't,' said Mrs Buckland. 'We have to get them from Brinton.'

'How d'you know they're free range?' asked the vicar.

'We take their word for it,' said Mr Buckland.

'I prefer to see the hens running about,' said the Vicar.

'There's a bus due in a quarter of an hour and you could be in Brinton in half an hour or so. Go to Barretts and ask them. But I ought to warn you that the probability is that they get them from someone else. Indeed, from a lot of other people, and you'd have to go touring the country to see the hens.'

'Not a bad idea,' said the vicar. 'If I have a half day off and if I were given all the addresses from which the eggs came I might go round and satisfy myself.'

'At that rate,' said Mrs Buckland, 'you'll want to go round to all the slaughter-houses to see that the thing's done decently and to all the farmers for the same reason. You'll have to give up saving our souls and spend most of your time tracing the history of the food that you eat. Have you ever understood why a kindly Creator brought us up to kill for food? Perhaps you'll preach on this some day.'

'I have,' said the vicar, 'but it's a very difficult subject and I wasn't very good. So I don't think you missed much.'

'Well, do it again,' said Mr Buckland. 'About Christmas time. Bring in turkeys and geese and all that. Not to mention a few sucking pigs.'

'Don't be beastly, Edward,' said Mrs Buckland. 'You know that I could easily become a vegetarian.'

'It's too expensive,' said Mr Buckland.

'Surely meat and poultry are more expensive?' said the vicar.

'Not unless you're going to live on potatoes,' said Mr Buckland. 'A vegetarian diet can in fact be very interesting and very varied, but it's devilish expensive if you're going to do it properly and anyway I'm a meat eater and don't want to.'

'And could I have half a pound of tea, please?' said the vicar.

'The usual?'

'Yes, please. Tell me this, Mary. I always make tea the same way and we always have the same tea. How is it that sometimes it's very nice and sometimes much less so? I make it with boiling water, I scald the pot, I dry it out, I infuse the tea with just a little boiling water to begin with. The water's freshly drawn, it's freshly boiled, it's made in the same pot. What's the reason for the difference?'

'If you use the same tea,' said Mrs Buckland, 'I can only assume that you slip up on something.'

'I expect I do occasionally,' said the vicar, 'but that can't be the reason because it happens too often and I'm very careful about making the tea.'

'Maybe your mouth or your digestion is not in order sometimes,' said Mr Buckland.

'But not my wife's too,' said the vicar. 'Because we nearly always agree whether it's a good cup or not.'

'It shows it doesn't do to be too particular,' said Mr Buckland. 'Perfectionists always run into trouble.'

'I wonder how Mr Gladstone likes his tea,' said Mrs Buckland.

'Mr Gladstone?' said the vicar.

'The bank robber,' said Mr Buckland. 'She's got him on the brain. I'm glad she hasn't got him in the spare room upstairs. I don't think he can be very particular at the moment how he gets his tea.'

'It must be awful to be on the run without a friend in the world,' said Mrs Buckland. 'To know that there's no one to whom you can turn for help. Even the vicar here would give him away to the police.'

'If he didn't knock me down first,' said the vicar. 'Your wife ought to get it into her romantic little head that people like Mr Gladstone can be very dangerous men.'

'They didn't hurt anybody when they broke into the bank,' said Mrs Buckland.

'It wasn't necessary,' said the vicar. 'I hope I don't think the worst of people but it's impossible to believe that they wouldn't have used violence if it had been necessary. A man with his hands on a fortune and his freedom at stake must be a desperate man. And another tin of that clear soup, please.'

During this conversation there had been background music from the radio. It was suddenly interrupted by a BBC announcer saying: 'Here is a news flash. The police believe that the escaped bank robber Gladstone is in a house in a street in Soho. The whole of the area has been cordoned off.'

'Bad luck, Mary,' said Mr Buckland, 'if you'd been a hostess in a Soho club you might have met him.'

'How awful for him to be cornered like that,' said Mrs Buckland. 'Wondering if every footstep is that of the police. Wondering if they are coming in through the window or through the front door. I've never seen a cornered animal, not even a rat. It must be a horrible sight. I should hate to.'

'But, Mary,' said the vicar, rather gently, 'he didn't have to take to a life of crime. He didn't have to escape after he was sentenced.'

'How would you like to be locked up for about twenty-five years?' said Mary.

'All right,' said the vicar. 'I can understand his wanting to escape and escaping, but why couldn't he have led an honest life like the rest of us? I don't mean that we're all completely honest. Of course we're not, but we don't rob each other too openly.'

'Who knows why anybody does anything?' asked Mrs Buckland. 'I fell in love with Edward when I was twenty-four. But why?'

'Sexual attraction,' said Mr Buckland.

'Partly,' said Mrs Buckland, 'but not entirely. There must have been a lot I liked about the rest of you.'

'But I don't quite know what that's got to do with Gladstone taking to crime as a form of living,' said the vicar.

'Perhaps he couldn't conform,' said Mrs Buckland. 'Perhaps he didn't like the present state of society. Perhaps he didn't like the fact that some people can live in comfort and some people live in grave discomfort. Is it right, vicar, that Mrs Winchcombe can give expensive dinner parties while some people live in damp, rat-infested places and haven't enough to eat? Is that right?'

'No,' said the vicar, 'it isn't. And every Government in this country, of whatever political flavour, is striving to improve things so that it doesn't happen. It is infinitely better than it was at the beginning of the century or, indeed, thirty years ago.'

'How many people,' said Mrs Buckland, 'don't get enough to eat? How many people still live in slums which ought to be condemned? Ten or twenty?'

'More than that,' said the vicar.

'A thousand? Ten thousand?'

'I don't know,' said the vicar. 'But certainly far too many.'

'Which is the worse?' said Mrs Buckland. 'That these thousands of people should live in such conditions while people like Mrs Winchcombe live in conditions of luxury and we live in conditions of considerable comfort or that Gladstone should steal a million pounds from a bank which has too much anyway?'

'Don't spoil the argument by saying that a bank has too much anyway,' said the vicar. 'I'm not an economist, but I have little doubt that most people in the country directly or indirectly owe their means of livelihood to the banks. That's the capitalist system. But if you went to Russia you aren't going to tell me that everyone there lives in at least some degree of comfort. The truth of the matter, of course, is that there is a great deal wrong with the world and every part of it. And terribly wrong with some parts of it. Far worse than in this country. Just because there are bad things going on in this country that doesn't justify someone who disapproves of it opting out from the social system and putting his hands in other people's pockets. Even if Gladstone were going to use the money for some very proper purpose, such as building old people's homes, even if he were a genuine Robin Hood we couldn't allow it or a state of lawlessness would emerge. But I don't think somehow that this particular bank robber is going to use his money to build houses for the homeless, do you?'

'I don't suppose he is,' said Mrs Buckland. 'No, I don't suppose it for a moment. But all I can think of at present is of the wretched man, cornered in some house in some street in Soho.'

CHAPTER FIVE

Cornered?

There was no doubt that the police must have felt pretty certain that Gladstone was cornered. From the ordinary person's point of view, particularly that of the motorist, chaos reigned. In Shaftesbury Avenue. In Soho. In Piccadilly Circus. In Piccadilly. In Charing Cross Road. For a quarter of a mile from the centre of the street where Gladstone was believed to be no person or vehicle was allowed to move without police permission. It was no good saying that you were a member of Parliament on the way to the House, or a barrister on the way to court, or a doctor on the way to perform an operation. The police were taking no chances. They may indeed have incurred the risk of contempt of Parliament by holding up one MP who said he was able to identify himself conclusively by documents, which he offered to produce.

'They might be forged,' said the police officer. 'Please don't think, sir, that I am suggesting for a moment that they are or that you are anybody except who you say you are. But I don't know John Gladstone by sight. You are of about the same age and the same height and I am under the strictest orders not to let anyone through. And, even if you weren't he, you might be taking a message from him to someone else.'

'Well,' said the MP, 'I'm glad that you are so thorough and I only hope you'll catch him.'

'We'll catch him all right,' said the policeman. 'If you'll excuse me, sir – ' And he moved away to deal with a gesticulating foreigner who hadn't the faintest idea of what it was all about.

Some people, of course, got a lot of excitement out of it without having to pay for it. Most of them found it interesting to begin with, but drivers who were held up in Shaftesbury Avenue for an hour and a half ceased to find it amusing, interesting or exciting but only wondered when the hell it would be over. Meantime the only vehicles that moved were police vehicles. Somehow or other by pushing, pulling, shoving, occasionally swearing, they managed to thread a way through to their destinations. Policemen on foot were everywhere, all of them with walkie-talkies. If they all talked at the same time it is difficult to imagine what the result would have been. Presumably as much chaos in the air as there was on the road. Only one other vehicle was let through – an ambulance. And even that was not allowed in before the driver had explained that he'd come from a hospital to call for a woman who was requiring an urgent abdominal operation. But they checked with Scotland Yard that a call had come from the hospital first.

Knowing that the police do not take very kindly to escaped bank robbers, some people wondered whether the ambulance was for the purpose of removing Gladstone's remains. Moreover, although John Gladstone had not in fact used any force, it was obvious that a man in his position on the run might well have obtained arms for the purpose of effecting his escape. At any rate the police who were proposing to arrest him were all armed. They managed to force a passage for the ambulance and to hold the crowd back while the stretcher bearers removed the body. Even then they raised the blanket just to make sure. Then they helped the ambulance to thread its way through the tangled mass of traffic and eventually towards St Thomas' Hospital. Meantime every single room in Old Compton Street was being searched for Gladstone. Policemen were watching from the roofs almost from the start so that no escape lay for him that way. After two and a half hours of public confusion and frantic searching by the police John Gladstone had not been found. The Chief Superintendent responsible for the operation spoke on the telephone to an assistant commissioner at Scotland Yard.

'There's no trace of him, sir,' he said. 'How long must we keep the cordon on? People are getting pretty browned off.'

'Damn the public,' said the assistant commissioner. 'Find Gladstone. It's all for their benefit and they must put up with it.'

But after two further hours of fruitless search the assistant commissioner agreed to the cordon being removed. It took another two hours for the traffic to disentangle itself.

Far away from the chaos Mary Buckland gave a private smile to herself in the looking glass and far away from Little Bacon, John Gladstone was flying to the South of France.

The information given to the police had indeed been correct, but Gladstone had arranged for his removal in a public service vehicle, the ambulance. The policeman had indeed lifted the blanket but had not liked to raise what he thought was a lady's skirt. And the telephone call from the hospital to Scotland Yard was a fake. There was something in what the judge had said about improving the standard of intelligence in the Force.

CHAPTER SIX

Mr Partridge on Crime

It was just about six months after Gladstone's escape that Mr Partridge arrived at Little Bacon. During those months there had been one or two references in the press to the bank robbery, when there were rumours that Gladstone was in different places in the world, but none of them ever came to anything. Mr Partridge eventually settled down very happily in Little Bacon. Most people liked him. He was up to the indifferent standard of the judge and the commander at croquet and he kept a very good cellar. It was, however, some time before he was invited to Broadway House. Mrs Winchcombe moved warily in her choice of friends and even acquaintances, and before you were invited by her to dinner you were surveyed, inspected and weighed in the balance. Anyone who made an effort to be accepted was immediately discarded. Mr Partridge certainly did not make this mistake. Apart from his first sudden call on the commander when he thought he was being shot at, he was extremely careful not to obtrude himself. He was very ready to accept an invitation and to return it but he never overplayed his cards. On the occasions when he met Mrs Winchcombe he was polite and friendly but a little reserved. Mrs Winchcombe liked this attitude and decided to find out whether Mr Partridge could be said to be an expert in any particular field. But all she could find out about the man was that he appeared to be well-to-do and to have retired early from some kind of business and to have a smattering of knowledge of most general subjects. Apart from a keen interest in wine she could find no particular aspect of life on which he purported to be an authority or anything like it. Wine would not do because there her husband was the expert and she did not propose to encourage rivals.

One day she put the question to him direct. It was during a croquet and tea party at the commander's.

'Mr Partridge,' she said, 'do you by any chance collect stamps?'

'Not really,' he replied. 'Of course as a boy I used to collect a few and my father, who did collect, left me a small collection, but I'm afraid I sold it.'

'I imagine you're not a countryman,' said Mrs Winchcombe. She of course knew of the episode about the bird scarers.

'I'm afraid not, though I must say I love the country and particularly I love it here.'

'A musician, by any chance?'

'I'm very fond of music, but I couldn't possibly call myself a musician. I know nothing about it.'

'I'll tell you frankly why I'm asking,' said Mrs Winchcombe. 'Most people in this neighbourhood – most of our friends that is – have some specialised knowledge of one subject or another. Have you no speciality?'

Mr Partridge thought for a moment. 'Well, I suppose, if you press me, I have. I have never looked upon it as a speciality, but there is an aspect of life in which I was professionally interested at one time. Although I no longer have any professional association with it, I still am deeply interested. I think most people are interested in the subject, but I do venture to think that owing to my professional associations with it I know a little bit more than other people. Would you care to guess what it is?'

'I dislike guessing,' said Mrs Winchcombe. 'If I get it right first go, I feel it's too easy and if I don't get it right first go I am made to feel a fool. What is it?'

'Crime,' said Mr Partridge.

Mrs Winchcombe was pleased.

'Indeed,' she said. 'But I didn't know you were in the law.'

'Not like the judge,' said Mr Partridge.

'You were a solicitor then?'

'Oh dear no!'

'Now don't start making me guess,' said Mrs Winchcombe. 'You know my views on that.'

'I used to go to prison a lot,' said Mr Partridge.

'Really?' said Mrs Winchcombe. 'In what particular capacity. Surely you weren't a prison officer or a policeman?'

'Oh no, but I came in contact with a lot of them. No, my association with prisons and criminals was first in one capacity and then in another. But it's a shame to tease you. I'm afraid I can't help it. Whenever the subject's raised and I say I've had professional experience of prisons I can see the person I am talking to wondering, however slightly, whether I was sent there for my own or for the public good or both. Well, I suppose I was.'

'You mean you've actually been sent to prison? For a driving offence, I suppose.'

'Oh no,' said Mr Partridge, 'not even a driving offence, I'm afraid. No, at one time I was a prison visitor and that gave me the idea of becoming a probation officer and I must say I found both experiences extremely rewarding. Mentally, I mean, not financially. Prison visitors, of course, don't get paid at all and the salary of probation officers is far too low.'

'And you really enjoyed seeing these thugs and cut-throats?'

'Very much,' said Mr Partridge. 'And I think most people would.'

'So I suppose,' said Mrs Winchcombe, 'you *can* describe yourself as an expert on crime. If you've met all these criminals, presumably you know the way they go about their business and why they turn to crime instead of to honest work and so on.'

'Yes,' said Mr Partridge. 'I think I know a good deal about that.'

'And do you follow cases much now?'

'Oh yes. From time to time I see that old friends of mine have been charged again and sometimes they suffer an injustice and are acquitted.'

'Are many guilty men acquitted?' asked Mrs Winchcombe.

'Nearly all of them,' said Mr Partridge.

'I don't understand. A lot of guilty men are convicted.'

'I put that rather badly,' said Mr Partridge. 'What I mean is this. Most people who are acquitted of serious offences – I don't mean driving offences or manslaughter as the result of a fight or that sort of thing – but serious offences, like robbery, blackmail, fraud, forgery, substantial thefts and so on – most of those people – nearly all of them – are guilty. But quite a lot are lucky and get off.'

'I must ask the judge about this,' said Mrs Winchcombe. 'Because that isn't justice.'

'Nobody suggests it is,' said Mr Partridge. 'But it's the best we can do. We try to make it impossible to convict the innocent. In order to do that we have to make the meshes of the net so wide that a lot of guilty fish can swim out.

This is most unfair on the public, but personally I have never been able to see an alternative.'

'Why do you feel so certain about this,' said Mrs Winchcombe.

'Because of my experiences,' said Mr Partridge. 'But I think you will find that the judge will agree with me. The only people who stand in danger of being convicted when they are innocent are confirmed criminals. The ordinary respectable person stands in no such danger. If you or I or any of our friends is ever charged with a serious offence you can be perfectly certain that we are guilty. To begin with, you see, the police have got to suspect that there's something suspicious about our behaviour. They have got to have some evidence that we've done something that we shouldn't have done. This is most unlikely unless in fact we've done something. I am quite sure nobody's ever made any enquiries about you, Mrs Winchcombe.'

'I should hope not.'

'Quite so. Nor about any of us. If by some mischance one of us were mistakenly thought to be implicated in a crime, our innocence would be disclosed at our first interview with a police officer. If in fact we were so bad at answering his questions that he thought his suspicions were correct, and investigated the case further with the result that we were actually charged, surely we'd be guilty. There would have to be an astonishing number of coincidences for it to be otherwise. The only way in which a respectable person ever runs the risk of being charged with a crime with which he'd nothing to do is if someone with a grievance against him tells lies about him or plants evidence on him. Well, how many times does this happen among respectable people? We don't like everybody we know. We may dislike some people and some people may dislike us. But how many of us have got a real enemy in the world? Someone who really wants us to suffer? Well, I suppose there are a few, but even that isn't sufficient. The enemy has got to be so malicious and determined or have such a warped mind that he or she is prepared to go to considerable lengths to try to procure a charge being preferred against us. So you can see for yourself that this is in the highest degree unlikely.'

'But you said there were some people who stood in danger of being convicted when they were innocent.'

'Oh yes,' said Mr Partridge. 'People with bad records. When a crime has been committed, unless the police have got some pretty good information as to the culprit, they first of all make out a list of possible criminals who might have done it. Then they investigate where they were on that occasion and so forth. In the result, they may find that there are half a dozen possible culprits. And they go down and interview them. Suppose the case is one of burglary. It might be that on the night in question burglar A was not committing the crime about which the police are questioning him but was committing another crime somewhere else. So when the police come along and ask questions, he tells them lies. Subsequently the police discover that they are lies. They challenge him and probably he then tells further lies. In the end the police ask themselves why this chap should lie if he didn't do it. The crime has been committed in the particular way in which this man commits his burglaries, so they charge him. They probably have a little evidence against him as well – enough to make him go into the witness box. And in the witness box he lies again and then probably he calls somebody to give false evidence of an alibi. The witness is cross-examined into a cocked hat by counsel for the prosecution and the man is duly convicted, although he was innocent. Of course one can't shed a great many tears for such a man because the reason he was convicted was that he was in fact committing another crime at the time. But of course there can be cases where the man lies about his movements not because he was committing a crime at the time but because he was doing something which, for example, he doesn't want his wife to know. He may perhaps have been out with another woman or something of that kind. His wife may strongly object to his gambling and he may have been on a racecourse. But naturally once you start telling lies to the police any suspicions which they originally had are considerably increased.'

'And you can't suggest any solution to the problem?'

'I'm afraid not. It must happen in every country. Human beings are very fallible. I'm not so much surprised at the mistakes we make as the number of mistakes which are not made. I'm not so much surprised at the number of criminals who are acquitted when in fact they are guilty, as at the number of men who deny their guilt but who are in fact guilty and are convicted.'

'The judge is always saying that the only solution is to increase the police force,' said Mrs Winchcombe.

'How right he is, but fortunately there is little chance of it happening.'

'Fortunately?' queried Mrs Winchcombe.

'Fortunately for those who break the law, I mean. I have so many friends among the law-breakers, people I really like – some of whom I think you would have liked – that I'm inclined sometimes, even now, to look at things from their point of view.'

'But why do you say they won't increase the Police Force?'

'They'd be frightened to,' said Mr Partridge. 'To begin with, the only way of increasing the Force substantially is by greatly increasing the pay. Then the left wing movement in the country is quite strong and many of them hate the police. You would find them walking up and down the country with banners with "No more pigs" on them. Well, it's the only solution I can think of – and there is no politician or statesman that I know of big enough to make the Government do something about it.'

'Well, Mr Partridge, this has been a most interesting conversation,' said Mrs Winchcombe. 'I do hope you will come and dine with us one evening.'

'I should enjoy it very much,' said Mr Partridge.

CHAPTER SEVEN

Suspicion

It was not long before Mrs Winchcombe arranged a dinner party to show off her new expert and during the party she soon found an occasion to bring in the subject of crime.

'Bertie,' she said, 'Mr Partridge tells me that a lot of guilty men are acquitted. Would you agree with that?'

'Certainly,' said the judge.

'And do you think that it's right?' asked Mr Partridge.

'Of course it's not right,' said the judge. 'It's injustice and injustice can never be right. But the world is full of injustice, and we have to choose the injustice we prefer most.'

'Look, Bertie,' said the commander, 'you have a legal profession consisting not only of judges but of barristers and solicitors as well. You have clerks and courts and I don't know what else. If I can run my destroyer without putting it on to a sandbank, why can't you run the ship of law in the same way?'

'But,' said the judge, 'commanders do put their destroyers on sandbanks sometimes. They do worse. They make all sorts of mistakes. I'm not saying for a moment that you did, but it happens. This is unavoidable with human beings. They take infinite care with spacecraft but they burned some wretched astronauts to death just the same.'

'Well,' said the commander. 'I've never run a ship on a sandbank. I've never had an accident with a ship. Nearly, once – no, twice, perhaps. That was all. No one was hurt. Nor was the ship. Are you saying that injustices are as infrequent in the courts as they were on my ship?'

The judge thought for a moment. 'Well,' he said eventually, 'I'm not. I think there's more injustice done in the courts than there is at sea. Or in the Army. Or in the Air Force. Or in any occupation which is mainly or partly physical, except on the roads of course, where people are maimed and killed to a horrifying and wholly unnecessary extent. That is injustice for you, if you like. The courts are nothing like as bad as the roads.'

'How often have you made a mistake, Bertie?' asked Mrs Winchcombe.

'I wouldn't know,' said the judge. 'Sometimes when the Court of Appeal have allowed an appeal from one of my judgments I think they've been wrong. I think probably I've more often made a mistake when there's been no appeal from me.'

'Well you shouldn't have,' said the commander.

'You seem to forget, George,' said the judge, 'that the fog of the law is very much worse than fogs you have at sea and very much more difficult to deal with. At least when you have a fog at sea you can stop. We have to go on. Courts of justice are concerned with ascertaining the truth and it's been said that truth lies at the bottom of a well. But wherever it lies it is sometimes extremely difficult to find. In some cases nobody knows what the truth is. In other cases some people are telling lies while others are saying something that's untrue although they believe it to be true. Then again some people are trying to tell the truth but are quite unable to do so owing to a lapse of memory or something of that kind. This is one of the things that the public never seems to realise. They expect judges always to be right and, when there's an injustice, they say it ought never to have happened. Well, of course, in a perfect community it wouldn't happen. In a perfect community there'd be no need for law, no need for judges, police or lawyers or anything of that kind. On the whole, I think the English system has adapted itself pretty well to the needs of the community. Of course the courts have always made mistakes and they always will. As for juries, in criminal cases they do their work very well on the whole, except in motoring cases. There they are so biased in favour of the motorist – because they visualise themselves in the dock one day for some serious motoring offence – that they often break their oaths when they acquit somebody who is plainly guilty. In other cases they are pretty careful but naturally they lean towards acquitting a person rather than convicting and this is quite right. I have tried cases where I have personally been sure of the prisoners' guilt, but the jury have acquitted them. I have no complaint of that at all. Twelve ordinary men and women were not satisfied about the men's guilt. Suspicion is not enough. Not even strong suspicion. You've got to be sure, and they weren't sure. I was, but they weren't. And I personally prefer that sort of injustice to the chance of an innocent man being convicted. That is a possibility that horrifies everyone. The lawyers as much as anyone else. So that's why we weight the scales in favour of the guilty man.'

'Well,' said Mrs Winchcombe, 'Mr Partridge and the judge seem to agree about this. What a pity. I thought we might have an argument.'

'In that case,' said Mr Partridge, 'might I suggest something with which the judge mightn't agree? May I ask you a question, judge?'

'Certainly.'

'How much do you know about the men you sentence for serious crimes?'

'Well,' said the judge, 'I know the circumstances of the crime and I know what the police and the probation officer tell me about the man's record and sometimes I get a witness as to character, the man's employer or the vicar or somebody of that sort.'

'But how much do you know of the man himself?' asked Mr Partridge. 'You've never met him.'

'Of course not,' said the judge. 'If I'd met him I couldn't try him.'

'Well, how can you know the right sentence to pass if you don't know the man? We're all different. The man you've got to deal with has committed a crime. But why? What makes him tick the wrong way. Why is he different from the rest of us?'

'Sometimes,' said the judge, 'a psychiatrist gives evidence.'

'I don't suppose you take much notice of that,' said Mr Partridge.

'I can't say that I do,' said the judge. 'I daresay it's my fault. Perhaps I think that many psychiatrists are inclined to use long words for comparatively simple matters. For example, they call a man whom I would just call "bad" a psychopathic personality.'

'What is bad?' asked Mrs Partridge.

'A man is bad,' said the judge, 'if he does things that no decent man would do.'

'That doesn't seem to get us very far, if you'll forgive my saying so,' said Mr Partridge. 'What does a decent man do?

There are all sorts of things we shouldn't do. We shouldn't take other people's property. We shouldn't knock people on the head. We shouldn't run off with other people's wives and so on. But even people who don't do any of those things are bad at heart sometimes.'

'Oh yes,' said the judge, 'we're all bad at heart sometimes. That's, for example, when we're tempted to do something that we oughtn't to do but the good man doesn't do it and the bad man does it. And if the "something" is against the law he must pay the penalty.'

'What penalty?' asked Mr Partridge. 'Prison doesn't do any good to most of the people who go there.'

'The fear of it does some good,' said the judge. 'Particularly to people who've never been there. I was never in favour of imprisonment for debt, but a very large number of debtors paid their debts rather than go to prison. In one year, for example, there may have been 180,000 orders sending people to prison unless they paid their debts by certain instalments. And you'd find that all but 5,000 or so of those people would pay. But I grant you that prison isn't a great deterrent to the regular criminal. It's no longer a horrible mystery to him. He knows all about it.'

'Mr Partridge,' said Mrs Winchcombe, 'says that murderers and all those thugs are really quite nice people.'

'Not exactly,' said Mr Partridge. 'I didn't say murderers. In fact I've never had anything to do with murderers. But the people you call "all those thugs", yes, some of them are very nice chaps. The only thing wrong with some of them is that they don't like work. They want a short cut to easy living and they take it. Of course the law doesn't approve and when they're caught they have to go to prison. But apart from that little failing, they are quite pleasant people.'

' "That little failing", as you call it,' said the judge, 'means that other people have to work twice as hard so that the rest of us may be able to live.'

'Not twice as hard, surely,' said Mr Partridge. 'Most people in the country are law-abiding. There are only 40,000 people in prison. 40,000 out of 50 million isn't one percent.'

'You say you haven't met any murderers,' said the commander. 'But have you met any of the big organisers of crime? For instance, the men who organised the Great Train Robbery or that bank robbery.'

'There are so many bank robberies,' said Mr Partridge. 'Which particular one do you mean?'

'When they got away with about two and a half million pounds and the man with the brains behind it escaped shortly afterwards. The same day as he was sentenced, as a matter of fact.'

'Oh, Gladstone, you mean,' said Mr Partridge. 'No, I've never met him or any of that type. For one thing they very rarely come to prison and, secondly, they're never on probation.'

'But don't they see prison visitors?' said Mrs Winchcombe.

'Oh, I suppose so,' said Mr Partridge, 'though they've never come my way. But I've met some members of the gang. As I've said, they're very nice chaps. The trouble is they all want short cuts to easy living.'

'I wonder where Gladstone is now?' said the vicar. 'A good many people have been wondering that for a long time,' said Mr Partridge. 'I believe he's supposed to be in the Argentine.'

'Oh?' said the judge. 'I haven't noticed that recently.'

'Oh, I haven't seen it recently,' said Mr Partridge, 'but about three or four months ago there was a small paragraph in the paper. D'you think they'll get him, judge?'

'How should I know,' said the judge. 'They don't consult me about these matters. But they usually do. I know the judge who tried him, as a matter of fact.'

'It makes a pretty good fool of the law,' said the commander, 'if the judge can give a man twenty-five years and within an hour the man's free.'

'I quite agree,' said the judge. 'But they can't have a regiment of soldiers to guard every prisoner. The police seem to have taken every precaution.'

'You don't think the police were parties to it then?' said Mr Partridge.

'I shouldn't think so for a moment,' said the judge. 'There is some corruption among the police, but very little indeed and in a case of this sort the police and the prison service would be very, very careful.'

'But not careful enough,' said the commander.

'You wouldn't expect a couple of fire engines to rescue the man.'

'I should have thought,' said the commander, 'that you must expect anything. Next time they may use a tank or a helicopter. You must always assume that the enemy will use any method. It was lack of efficiency and imagination. That's the trouble. I don't mean just the police, but all of us really. People don't think ahead enough. If it comes to that they don't think enough.'

'Well, I think the younger generation,' said the judge, 'are pretty good. They're much more enquiring than we were. They've got a pretty high standard of intelligence and, apart from the lunatic fringe, I personally find them anxious to help in the world and well-mannered.'

Mrs Winchcombe was sorry that she had not been able to do more with the new arrival, but on the whole, she felt that she had made a reasonable contribution in producing Mr Partridge.

Mr Partridge himself was delighted. It was not long before he started to entertain the whole neighbourhood, and very well he did it too. His invitations were rarely refused, provided the person invited was able to come.

'My dear vicar, why don't you preach on port one day?' Mr Partridge asked on one of these occasions.

'Well,' said the vicar, 'I've never really thought about it. What do you suggest I could say?'

'It improves with age,' said Mr Partridge, 'which is more than I do, though I should. You tell me so one Sunday.'

'I'll think about it,' said the vicar. 'I must say this port is particularly delicious. May I ask what it is?'

'It's Cockburn '27. Some people say it's gone over, but in my view that's nonsense. It's jealousy really, because they haven't got any. What do you say, commander? D'you pass this port?'

Lower down the table a guest was heard to remark, very quietly, 'I wish he would.'

'Well, if you want the truth, my dear boy,' began the commander.

'No, commander,' interrupted Mr Partridge, 'We're all friends here so I don't want the truth. I find the truth disturbing. There's another text for you, vicar. The truth that disturbs. Mrs Lauderdale, you're not drinking anything.'

'I'm driving, you see,' she said.

'Give me a pencil and paper,' said Mr Partridge, 'and I'll soon tell you whether you can have any more. Now, what's your weight?'

'I'm afraid that comes under the heading of the truth that disturbs,' said Mrs Lauderdale.

'Well, I've got it all here,' said Mr Partridge. 'Really, I have. If I know your weight and your age and whether you drank anything before you came here and so on, I can tell you almost exactly what milligrammes you have in your blood.'

'I'm sorry,' said Mrs Lauderdale, 'I'm not going to tell you.'

There was a sudden slightly embarrassing silence. Mrs Lauderdale was aware of her age and her weight, but was not particularly anxious to make them public property.

She broke the silence by saying, 'Perhaps I can ask you a question or two, Mr Partridge. What exactly was your business before you retired? I hope you don't mind my asking. You are retired, aren't you?'

'Yes,' said Mr Partridge. 'I am retired. What a charming dress that is.'

'But before you retired what did you do?' asked Mrs Lauderdale. 'You must have done it well to be able to give us such excellent port.'

'Oh, I earned my living,' said Mr Partridge. 'Nothing very interesting, but I'm glad to say profitable. But I must confess I much prefer not to have to earn my living. I am idle by nature.'

'Was it your father's business by any chance?' asked Mrs Lauderdale.

'No,' said Mr Partridge, 'it was not. Nor my mother's. Nor my brother's. Nor my aunt's. Nor my uncle's. Does that satisfy you?' There was another slightly embarrassing silence.

'You did ask her weight and age, you know, Partridge,' said the commander.

'Thank you, commander,' said Mrs Lauderdale. 'I'm quite capable of looking after myself.'

When the party was over the commander asked the judge if he'd mind going for a short walk. 'I feel I want a breath of air,' he said.

'Of course,' said the judge, 'I'd be delighted.' They walked away from the house. 'That was a good party,' said the judge.

'Very,' said the commander. 'But don't you think there's something a little bit odd about Partridge? I like him and he gives excellent dinner parties, but who is he and where does he come from? He came here six months ago, but apart from the fact that he says that he was once a prison visitor and a probation officer we don't know a thing about him. He tells us nothing.'

'Why should he?' said the judge. 'Some people are reticent about themselves. I like to tell people about my days at the Bar. You like to talk about your Navy days. The vicar will talk about his days as a curate. But there are people who haven't been happy in their youth or in their work or, indeed, in their later days. And when they at last get into a situation when they can really enjoy themselves they prefer not to talk about the past.'

'That's all very well, but the fellow might at least say what he did. Mrs Lauderdale asked him point blank.'

'No old school tie, d'you mean?'

'Oh, don't be ridiculous. I don't mind where the chap was at school. But what did he do? I shouldn't be ashamed if I'd been a greengrocer. Perhaps he was a wine merchant. He could easily have been that to judge by the drink he provides. But why shouldn't he say so?'

'It may be a form of snobbery,' said the judge. 'After all, you're a sailor, I'm a lawyer, and there's the doctor and the vicar and so on. He associates with us on terms of equality. He may not like to feel that in status he's rather below us. I know that's all out of date and that nobody's below anybody and nobody's above anybody today. But there are still people who believe in status. Some of the people below and a good many of the people above.'

'But why shouldn't he give us some inkling whether he made bricks or was a bookmaker or what he did to enable him to live in such comfort? He certainly didn't get it out of his savings as a probation officer.'

'What are you leading up to?' said the judge. 'He's good company, he's an excellent neighbour, and he's got one of the best cellars in the neighbourhood. Why should we mind what he did in the past?'

'I've just got a feeling about it,' said the commander. He said nothing for a moment and then added: 'I'd better come straight to the point, but I'm wondering if he's that chap who escaped, Gladstone.'

'Gladstone?' exclaimed the judge. 'Why on earth should you think that?'

'If you want to avoid detection, isn't the best way to hide to go into a community and to sort of fade into it? And he's got a beard.'

'So have you, George.'

'It's quite usual in the Navy,' said the commander. 'I daresay it's all nonsense, but I shouldn't have been happy if I hadn't mentioned it to you. Let's keep a lookout. You tell me if you notice anything strange.'

'Now you mention it,' said the judge, 'I did notice something strange.'

'Oh?'

'It won't back up your suspicions. The contrary. D'you remember the first thing that he did when he came here?'

'I can't say that I do.'

'He asked the way to the nearest police station.'

'That could be bravado.'

'I should think that was carrying things a bit too far,' said the judge. 'You say he wants to fade into the neighbourhood. The first thing he does is to ask the way to the nearest police station. I should think that would be the last thing he'd want to do.'

'I'm not sure,' said the commander. 'The sooner he meets the local bobby, from his point of view the better.'

'Well, what are you proposing to do about it?' asked the judge. 'Take his fingerprints?'

'Don't be absurd, Bertie. I'm sorry I told you now. But I thought at least you as a judge wouldn't laugh at me. It's just a feeling I've got and I wanted to tell somebody and you seemed the obvious person to tell.'

'Sorry, George,' said the judge. 'I don't mean to hurt your feelings. It's easy enough to make out a case against somebody if you set your mind on it.'

'How d'you mean?'

'Well,' said the judge. 'I wasn't at your wedding. I've never seen your marriage certificate. How do I know that you're not living in sin – if that's what it's still called.'

'Fair enough,' said the commander, 'and I haven't seen yours.'

'I wasn't being serious,' said the judge. 'I expect there's a picture in the *Tatler* of you and the bridal party outside the church. With crossed swords, probably.'

'There was, as a matter of fact,' said the commander.

'I hadn't thought of it when I said it,' went on the judge, 'but it's not really such an absurd suggestion. D'you know, Betty and I seriously considered whether to get married or not. This was when I was at the Bar. She used to make quite a bit out of her writing. Well, as you know, it's cheaper from the tax point of view for two people to live in sin than to get married and then they can each have a separate income and a separate assessment.'

'D'you mean you seriously considered not getting married? I'm not being offensive. I can imagine *you* dispensing with the ceremony, but I can't imagine Betty. She is what I would call a really good woman in the best sense of the word.'

'You're quite right,' said the judge, 'she is, and nothing would induce her to live with me without being married to me in the eyes of God. But as I was a budding young barrister in those days I did seriously consider this scheme. I had two alternatives in mind, as a matter of fact. One was to go through the whole of the ceremony and then to refuse to sign the register. The idea being that we would then be married in the eyes of God, which was all that mattered, and dispense with the civil ceremony. But I came to the conclusion that the difficulty there would be that we had in fact been married in accordance with the rites of the Established Church and there were plenty of witnesses to this. And probably the only people who would lose by doing it in that way would be ourselves, that's to say, we'd never be able to get a passport or anything of that kind because we would never have a marriage certificate, but when we came to the Inland Revenue they would say that we were in fact married. So then I had another idea. That was to invite to the wedding a very few friends, who would be in the plot, to have no music and to arrange that all friends should quietly slip away before the ceremony was completed.'

'Why no music?' asked the commander.

'Because then the organist would not be a witness.'

'But you need two witnesses,' said the commander.

'True enough,' said the judge, 'but it's arguable, I suppose, that the parson himself could be a witness. Well, provided the parson didn't notice the people slipping away and went on with the ceremony and pronounced us man and wife in the eyes of God, we'd be properly married from our point of view, but it wouldn't be a valid ceremony because there weren't two witnesses.'

'Why didn't you do it?' asked the commander.

'In the end we didn't think it worth it,' said the judge. 'Taxation wasn't so high then.'

'If you were single now, would you do it?' asked the commander.

'Oh no,' said the judge. 'One of the penalties of being a judge is, first, that you've got to behave yourself and, secondly, that you shouldn't do anything in your private life out of the ordinary. Nothing to get publicity or to cause talk. And that would certainly have caused talk and people would have said that it was unsatisfactory for a judge to get out of paying tax in that way. But, coming back to Mr Partridge, you've never seriously thought that he might be Mr Gladstone?'

'I suppose not really,' said the commander. 'But you know what it is. When there's a wanted man about the place and you walk through the streets of London, you see him in every other face.'

'But there hasn't been a hue and cry for Gladstone recently,' said the judge.

'That's true,' said the commander, 'but I'll tell you what has happened. Gladstone has been mentioned once or twice and sometimes I wondered what had become of him. And then – I don't know if you remember when he escaped we talked quite a lot about what a chap like that does when he escapes – I suddenly started playing with the idea of his coming among us. Well, of course there's only one stranger here and that's Partridge. I'd been thinking about him idly at the time of Hester Winchcombe's dinner party. And then his deliberate refusal to say what his business was did strike me as odd. So I thought I'd mention it to you.'

'Well, let me know if you think of anything else,' said the judge. 'Your thoughts aren't really strong enough to be called suspicions. I don't believe for a moment that they're correct, but equally I can't say definitely that they're wrong. I'll keep my eyes and ears open – before he becomes too close a friend.'

The matter wasn't mentioned again for several weeks. The fact that he didn't talk about it again to anybody else made the commander brood upon the matter rather more than he would have otherwise done. Eventually he decided that he must get it off his chest again and he introduced the subject when he and the vicar and the judge were together one day.

'What d'you think about Partridge, Harvey?' he asked.

'A very nice fellow.'

'We're all agreed on that,' said the commander, 'but what d'you think he used to do for a living? How did he make his money?'

'I've no idea,' said the vicar. 'I believe somebody did ask him but he didn't say.'

'Why d'you think he didn't say?'

'Because he didn't want to, I suppose,' said the judge.

'Why didn't he want to?' insisted the commander. 'Why d'you think he didn't want to, vicar?'

'I've never considered the matter,' said the vicar, 'but, as you ask me, it may have been something he didn't like to talk about, such as contraceptives for example. If my father had made his money that way I don't suppose I should be all that keen on mentioning it at a dinner party.'

'What d'you say to that, George?' asked the judge. 'I confess I hadn't thought of that,' said the commander. 'It is possible, I suppose, that he was engaged in some trade which at any rate usedn't to be mentioned in polite society. Twenty years ago you wouldn't have found the vicar talking about contraceptives quite openly.'

'Or it might have been armaments,' said the vicar. 'Look at the amount of crime there is in the United States, partly because anybody can buy a revolver whenever he wants to. I shouldn't feel particularly proud if I'd made my money by selling revolvers to the United States of America.'

'Of course,' said the judge, 'his mother might have been a very successful brothel-keeper.'

'Why his mother?' asked the commander. 'It could have been his father.'

'Come to that, it might have been the whole family,' said the vicar.

'Well, he could have invented something,' said the commander. 'He could have said he was in the rubber trade or something of that sort.'

'Then somebody might have asked him if he made sponges or the like. I think that probably is the reason he doesn't like talking about his business. It was something of that kind and once you start answering questions it's very difficult not to say exactly what you did.'

'And another thing occurs to me,' said the judge. 'He may have been involved in some case which at the moment we don't associate with the name of Partridge but if he told us what he'd done the penny might suddenly drop and we'd realise that there'd been a lot of publicity about it of a very unsatisfactory kind and, now he's lived it down, he wants to start afresh.'

'D'you remember any case with the name of Partridge in it, Bertie?' asked the commander.

'I can't say that I do at the moment,' said the judge, 'but that doesn't mean a thing. I forget names almost as fast as

I hear them. But has something else happened to increase your suspicions?'

'Not really,' said the commander. 'But the more I think about it the more I begin to wonder. In fact I went to the library and turned up a copy of *The Times* which had got Gladstone's picture in it. I'm not much of an artist, but I sent for a copy of that number of *The Times* and I added Partridge's beard and moustache to the picture. It's not unlike him, you know. I've got it here if you'd care to see it.'

'Certainly,' said the judge. 'Let's have a look.' The commander brought out the picture and the others had a look at it.

'You draw quite well really, George,' said the judge. 'I'd no idea you were so good.'

'Don't you think it's like him?' asked the commander.

'A bit,' said the judge.

'Well, George,' said the vicar, 'what do you expect us to do? Take his fingerprints?'

'Why shouldn't we?'

'Really, George. You go and dine with a man and eat his food and drink his wine and then take his fingerprints?'

'I don't mean openly,' said the commander. 'We could give him a sticky plate to catch hold of or something.'

'I think that's rather worse,' said the judge. 'If we're really suspicious of the man we ought to go to the police, but, if we do, they'll come down and see him. They'll have to. It'll be their duty to do so, and then he'll know that one of us has made the suggestion. That'll be nice, won't it? He won't know which of us.'

'Well,' said the commander, 'we'll look pretty good fools if it really is Gladstone.'

'I was just about to say,' said the judge, 'that we'd look rather worse than pretty good fools if he isn't. You don't really believe that he is, do you?'

'I don't know,' said the commander. 'I'm worried.'

'Then go and ask him,' said the judge.

'What d'you expect him to say?' said the commander. 'Of course he'd deny it and the next day he'd be gone and you know who would get the most blame.'

'You mean me,' said the judge. 'The judge who didn't notice. Yes. You're quite right. If Gladstone has settled down among us as Partridge we shall be a laughing stock and I'll get most of the blame.'

'But, Bertie,' said the commander, 'it's rather worse than being a laughing stock. Here's this man who's stolen vast sums and has been sent to prison for twenty-five years settling calmly among us, we suspect he may be the wanted man, we tell him so and he disappears. We've got a duty to catch the man.'

'Of course we have,' said the judge, 'if he is the man. But I'd want a lot more material before I did anything about it. If you're unhappy, George, you go to the police.'

'Would you come with me?'

'No, certainly not.'

'Would you, Harvey?'

'No, I'm afraid not.'

'You're in his favour because of what he puts in the plate on Sundays.'

'Really, George, that's a disgraceful suggestion.'

'I don't know why,' said the commander. 'D'you know where the money comes from?'

'I saw you give a pound last week,' said the judge. 'Where did that come from, George?'

'Out of my pension,' said the commander. 'I can't afford it. But five pounds every week. That's a very different thing.'

'How on earth d'you know that Partridge gives five pounds every week, George? Are you watching him the whole time?'

'When I get the chance,' said the commander, 'yes.'

'Shouldn't you be praying?' asked the vicar.

'Of course I should,' said the commander, 'but I can't pray the whole time. I don't pray during the sermon, for example, except sometimes for it to end. Not in your case, of course, Harvey.'

'During the collection,' said the judge, 'you should be singing a hymn.'

'I am,' said the commander, 'but that doesn't stop me keeping my eyes open.'

'I think your next sermon, Harvey,' said the judge, 'should be on charity. I hope you'll look at George when you preach it. 'Well, I'll tell you what I'll do, George. It's obvious that it's getting on your nerves and will become an obsession if we're not careful. I'll take him to court with me one day and over lunch I'll ask him as many questions as I can think of which are consistent with courtesy. Now will that satisfy you?'

'I don't know,' said the commander, 'until I hear the answers. But it'll certainly be something. When will you take him?'

'It depends on when he can come. Any time from now on.'

CHAPTER EIGHT

A Visit to Court

A week later the judge suggested to Mr Partridge that he might care to come to court with him one day and Mr Partridge, after a moment's hesitation, said that he would love to do so. They eventually fixed on a date and on the day they went off together in the judge's car. The judge started his cross-examination over lunch. He wondered if Partridge ever became bored now that he was retired and had nothing to do.

'Bored?' said Partridge. 'Good heavens, no. I've got my garden and my books and my recollections. And I've got my wine. And what with my friends and acquaintances in the neighbourhood I've very little time indeed for anything else. I couldn't do a job anyway even if I wanted to. I'm not qualified – except as a probation officer. And I'm not keen on starting that again.'

'You seem very comfortably off, if I may say so,' said the judge, 'for a man who's not qualified.'

'I'm glad to say that I am,' said Partridge.

'If you'll forgive me asking,' said the judge, 'what sort of work did you do?'

'Frankly, judge, I didn't like work. I scrounged around, you know. I managed to pick up a living here and there.

What about your early days at the Bar. How did you manage?'

'It wasn't at all easy,' said the judge, 'in those days. When I started, it took a long time to earn a decent income. But my parents helped me.'

'I had no parents,' said Partridge. And there was silence for a moment. 'If you want to know,' he went on, 'I was brought up in an institution.'

'I'm sorry,' said the judge. 'I shouldn't have been so inquisitive.'

'There's no need to apologise,' said Partridge. 'I'm a bit shy about it, I suppose. That's why I try and keep off the subject when anyone asks. It's silly, really. There's nothing to be ashamed of in being brought up in an institution. It wasn't my fault.'

'Of course it wasn't,' said the judge. 'A lot of successful men have started in the same way. And if I may say so, you seem to have been one of them.'

'I don't get my name into the papers,' said Partridge. 'But I've managed.'

'I think it's most creditable, if I may say so,' said the judge. 'And no doubt that's one of the reasons you became a probation officer. To help people who've been brought up like you have but have not made such a success of it.'

'Possibly. I never thought about it. I've always had just one ambition, even I may say when I was still a probation officer.'

'And what's that?'

'To live as I'm living now. Comfortably and happily, with a warm home, plenty of food and drink, lots of friends and nothing to do except garden, read and so forth. Most young men set their sights a bit higher. If it isn't Prime Minister or Lord Chancellor it's something of the kind. I never did. I did at one time want to help my fellow men. That's why I went into the probation service. But I'm afraid I was too selfish for that. I wanted more for myself. I wanted comfort and happiness. And I couldn't have the second without the first. I lived most uncomfortably as a probation officer, I must say.'

'Well, I'm delighted,' said the judge, 'that you've achieved your ambitions and I'm sure you deserve to have done so.'

'Orphan boy makes good,' said Mr Partridge.

'Oh, please,' said the judge, 'I'm really very sorry. I do hope I haven't embarrassed you.'

'Well, to tell you the truth,' said Partridge, 'you did start to embarrass me and then I thought it would be a good thing to get it off my chest. I'm not entirely a fool, you know. It isn't only magistrates and judges who can spot the truth.'

'I often can't spot it,' said the judge.

'No?' queried Partridge.

'Most certainly,' said the judge. 'There are judges who say they can always tell when a man or woman is telling the truth but I'm not one of them. The truth does have a habit of coming out in most cases, but not always.'

'Well,' said Partridge, 'I know what some of you have probably been saying behind my back. Asking who my father was, what I did for a living and how I made all my money and that sort of thing, and I did find it a bit hurtful. But fortunately my ambition has come to my assistance. I love my house. I love the neighbourhood. I'm very fond of all you chaps, so I became determined to ride the storm. I'm not going to give in, I said to myself. They can ask as much as they like but I'm going to pretend not to hear. But I must say I'm very grateful to you for bringing me to court today. It's given me a chance that I'll always be grateful for.'

'Well, I'm glad too,' said the judge. 'Would you mind if I told the others what you've told me?'

'Mightn't they look down on me?'

'I'm sure they wouldn't. On the contrary.'

'They might be sorry for me, which would be worse.'

'I don't think so. I think they'd just be ashamed of themselves and do everything they can to make you as happy as possible. That's human nature, you know. People who've done something wrong do want to make up for it if they can. But I'm talking as though we spend most of our time wondering who you were and where you came from and so on. That isn't so, I assure you. One or two of us have just wondered, that's all.'

Shortly afterwards the judge's clerk came in and said that counsel would like a word with the judge. The judge told his clerk to show them in.

'I expect they've settled the case or want my help in settling it or something of that kind,' said the judge to Partridge. 'I'll ask them if they mind your being here. I don't suppose they will. If they do, I'll have to get the clerk to take you to a waiting room.'

'I quite understand,' said Partridge.

A few minutes later two counsel came in. 'Come in Bentham. Come in, Green,' said the judge. 'This is my friend, Mr Partridge. Please sit down.' They all said "How d'you do", and then the judge asked them if they minded Mr Partridge remaining.

'Certainly not,' said Bentham. 'As a matter of fact he's the reason we've come. I only brought Green in because I knew you wouldn't see one of us without the other, and I've been wondering all the morning about Mr Partridge. I know we've met somewhere and I can't think where and if I go back home without having asked I shan't sleep all night.'

'How interesting,' said the judge.

'Well,' said Mr Partridge, 'I don't think I know you, Mr – er – did you say Mr Bentham?'

'That's right,' said Bentham. 'Haven't I appeared for you or against you in some case?'

'I've never had a case,' said Partridge, 'except obstruction by a motor car and I did that myself.'

'It's very odd,' said Bentham. 'I'm sure we've met. Would you think it very rude of me if I asked you if you've always had a beard and a moustache? Were you once clean-shaven and is that it?'

'Well, Bentham,' said the judge with a little asperity. 'I don't know what Mr Partridge thinks about it, but I should think it very rude of you. You're not cross-examining one of your witnesses now, you know.'

'I'm extremely sorry, judge,' said Bentham. 'I didn't mean to give you or Mr Partridge the slightest offence.'

'I'm not in the least offended,' said Partridge. 'No, I've had a beard and a moustache for many years.'

'You've never been on a jury I suppose?' asked Bentham.

'Yes, I was once, as a matter of fact.'

'At the Old Bailey?'

'Yes.'

'You had a beard then?'

'Certainly.'

'Perhaps that's it,' said Bentham. 'Beards are fairly rare on juries and on occasions when I address a jury I always try and find one intelligent-looking person to address. And it may be that was you, sir, and I've remembered you ever since.'

'It may be that it was, Bentham,' said the judge, 'but if that's all you wanted, I think you'd better get back to court.'

'Of course,' said Bentham. 'I'm so sorry to have kept you, judge. Goodbye, sir.'

'Goodbye,' said Partridge, 'and I'm so sorry I couldn't help you any more.'

The two counsel left.

'Confounded impudence,' said the judge. Had it not been for the commander's suspicions and their discussions about them and had it not been for the information which Partridge had recently confided in him the judge would not have been so touchy.

'I don't think he meant any harm,' said Partridge. 'I should feel like that myself. It's infuriating when you feel you know someone and you can't put a name to him or her.'

'Well, it's very nice of you to take it that way,' said the judge. 'But I still think it was damn cheek. Now I suppose we'd better get back into court.'

'Will you think it very rude of me,' said Partridge, 'if I don't come in this afternoon? I've been immensely interested in everything I've heard, but the beer which you've been good enough to give me for lunch has given me rather a headache and perhaps, if you don't mind, I'll sleep it off. That looks rather a comfy chair.'

'Of course,' said the judge. 'Shall I get the usher to give you a cup of tea?'

'Oh no, thank you very much,' said Partridge. 'I think forty winks is all I need and it wouldn't look well for me to indulge in them when I was sitting next to you on the bench.'

'I shut my eyes sometimes,' said the judge, 'but if I do, I'm always very careful to say something with my eyes still shut so as to show that I haven't been sleeping.'

Partridge went to the armchair and the judge went into court and resumed the case which he had been trying. It was an ordinary accident case and the evidence continued in the normal way. The plaintiff said that the defendant was travelling at over sixty miles an hour while the defendant said that he had only just pulled out of a lay-by and had not reached top gear. Both parties had independent witnesses. In fact all those independent gentlemen had seen was the resultant crash. They had heard a bang and looked up. But by the time they came into court they had seen everything from start to finish. One of them appeared to be able to look right and left at the same time. Counsel asked him a question. But the judge heard neither question nor answer.

For the first time in his life the judge had not been paying proper attention to the evidence. His mind had suddenly become obsessed with the fact that Partridge did not want to come into court that afternoon and had made a fairly flimsy excuse for not doing so. It was, of course, perfectly possible that he'd heard enough in the morning, that he wasn't particularly interested in courts and that he found the proceedings rather boring but didn't like to say so and had feigned a headache. Of course he might actually have a headache. But it was an odd coincidence that he didn't want to come into court when counsel had said that he thought that he recognized him. Was he staying out of court in order to prevent counsel from having a better look at him? The judge had then remembered the photograph in the paper upon which the commander had added a moustache and beard. No lawyer likes coincidences. Of course they occur in life, but seldom when the guilt or innocence of a person depends upon them. Usually a coincidence is simply a matter of interest. You find that the man sitting next to you in the train was brought up in the village where you were born; and as the train is travelling across Russia at the time, it is undoubtedly an extraordinary coincidence. But what of it? No one's guilt or innocence depends upon it. But when the jury's verdict does depend upon whether a man who was suspected of breaking into a car and stealing a portable wireless set which had a scratch on it, which the owner was able to identify, had himself bought a wireless set of exactly the same make second hand in the market with a similar scratch on it, and when a faint fingerprint on the car appears to have been that of the man concerned, the jury are more likely to think that he was guilty of the crime with which he was charged than that by pure coincidence he had bought a similar set to that owned by the chief witness for the prosecution and that it had been scratched in exactly the same way as the set which he was said to have stolen.

So here was a man with a beard and a moustache, certainly resembling at least to some extent an escaped bank robber, a man who seemed reluctant to say how he'd made his money, who had come into their neighbourhood six months after the bank robber had escaped and when counsel said he thought he recognized him apparently did not want to be seen by that counsel again. Instead of thinking about the evidence given by the defendant's swivel eyed witness, the judge was wondering whether there might not be much more in what the commander had suspected than he himself had thought possible. Then he pulled himself together.

'What was that last answer of the witness?' he asked.

'His last answer,' said counsel, 'was No.'

That did not tell the judge very much and he was compelled to ask what the question had been.

'I asked him if in addition to being able to look both ways at the same time he had eyes in the back of his head.'

'Thank you, Mr Bentham,' said the judge, and proceeded to write down almost mechanically "I have not got eyes in the back of my head." 'Very well then,' he said, 'your next question, please.'

The judge managed to go on and try the case properly, although whenever he got a moment to think outside the case he was wondering how he could speak to Bentham without asking him to come into his room. Eventually he decided that at the end of the case before he rose he would beckon both counsel to come and speak to him on the bench. There was nothing particularly unusual about this. If the judge wanted to have a quick word with counsel he would sometimes do this to save giving them the trouble of having to come into his room. But when the clock reached a quarter past four Bentham solved the problem for him.

'Your Honour,' he said, 'would it be very inconvenient for you to tell me how late you propose to sit? I have a conference in chambers which I am anxious to attend.'

'Well,' said the judge, 'it would be a pity to adjourn this case now. We should be able to finish it in half an hour, don't you think? Unless that will be too inconvenient for you.'

'Very well, your Honour,' said Bentham. 'I quite agree that it would be a hardship on the parties to adjourn the case. By all means let us try and finish it now. Will your Honour forgive me if I rush away at the end?'

'Of course,' said the judge, and realised that his chance of having a word with Bentham that day had gone.

When the case was over the judge went back to his room and found Partridge sitting in the chair reading the paper just like any honest man. Within a couple of seconds or even less (the mind can work so quickly) the judge suddenly had a revulsion of feeling in favour of Partridge.

Here was this man who had made good after being brought up in an institution without the advantage of parental love which he himself had had. And now because the man wore a beard and a moustache he was trying to make him into a dangerous criminal. How grossly unfair.

'Did you have a nice nap?' he asked.

'Splendid,' said Mr Partridge. 'My headache's entirely gone. I do hope you didn't mind my not coming into court.'

'Good gracious, no,' said the judge, 'although you might have been interested in the conflict of evidence in an accident case. I think it's silly to try the cases. There ought to be national insurance instead.'

Next morning the judge received a letter from Bentham.

'Dear Judge,' it read, 'I'm so sorry for embarrassing your guest today and I do agree that it was very bad manners on my part. I apologise to you again and I hope you will convey my apologies to Mr Partridge. It was simply that I felt so sure that I'd met him before that I couldn't resist asking. As a matter of fact I find that I'm quite wrong. By a pure coincidence I saw in one of today's papers a picture of the man I thought your friend was and it was somebody quite different. If I may say so, I always enjoy appearing in front of you and I do hope you will overlook my gaucherie.
With kindest regards,
Yours sincerely,
Alfred Bentham.'

The judge was pleased to receive the letter for two reasons. First, he never liked difficulties with counsel. The Bar and the Bench get on extremely well together on the whole and no one likes the occasional skirmishes which take place between them. The second reason he was pleased was that at first reading it confirmed entirely his opinion of Partridge. Then suddenly he had a thought. 'I wonder if there was a picture of Gladstone in the paper yesterday,' he said to himself.

CHAPTER NINE

A Chat in the Shop

There are various types of judges. The best type never comes to a final conclusion until he's heard the whole of the evidence and the arguments. Naturally in a plain case his mind is bound to tend towards being on the side of the party who is obviously in the right. But even in such cases he has such control over his mind that he is able to keep it open almost until the last word has been said on the subject. The worst type of judge comes to an early conclusion when there has been insufficient evidence and insufficient argument. Having come to this conclusion he tries to steer the case in such a way that in the end the conclusion seems obvious. But sometimes in the course of doing this he is suddenly brought up against something which he had never thought of and he is so affected by this and sometimes so shocked that instead of being in favour of the plaintiff he immediately becomes in favour of the defendant. In such cases he usually runs the case harder for the defendant than he ran it for the plaintiff in the first instance. And thereafter the unfortunate plaintiff who, to begin with, thought the judge was all sweetness and light finds to his horror that the blue-eyed boy in the eyes of the judge is now the defendant. So he feels even more disappointed when he loses the case than if his hopes had never been raised in the first instance. The experienced advocate dealing with such a judge knows what to do. When the judge makes it appear at an early stage that he is in favour of the plaintiff he bides his time. If he immediately tried to change the judge's view, it would probably only strengthen it. Possibly even to such an extent that he would feel unable to change it. So counsel waits until he has the opportunity of making a very telling point indeed on behalf of the defendant and from that moment he has the judge in his pocket because consciously or unconsciously, a judge will not like to perform too many *volte faces* in the same case.

Judge Ward was not one of the best or the worst judges but he tended towards being in the lower half of the league table. So in the present case he had started off strongly in favour of Mr Partridge. His whole judicial instinct objected to the man being suspected for wholly insufficient reasons. Then when he suddenly thought that there was cause for suspicion he went over to the other side and really began to wonder whether Partridge was not Gladstone. After he had received the shock of learning, according to Partridge, that he was brought up in an institution and feeling rather conscience-stricken about his suspicions, they were suddenly strengthened by Bentham's letter.

He was starting to find the whole thing rather embarrassing and worrying. But now at last he thought he had found the touchstone. If the photograph to which Bentham referred was indeed that of Gladstone, that was an end of the matter. He would go straight to the police and let the law take its course. Conversely, if it was not, he would endeavour to rid himself of suspicion altogether. He decided not to tell anyone of the development but to investigate the matter himself. He looked at the previous day's *Times* and *Telegraph*. There were no photographs in either of them to which Bentham could have been referring. So he went to the village store and saw Mrs Buckland. Her husband had gone to Brinton.

Newsagents as a whole are a pretty tolerant body. The boldest customers or potential customers can do almost anything with them. They can pick up *The Dog Breeder* just to see whether the particular article they want to read is in it and put it down a little the worse for wear when they find that it is not. They can do the same with several other papers and magazines and finally go away having bought nothing. The less bold do this more furtively and the weak-kneed ask if they may look. But naturally it is quite different in the local shop. There few people would have the slightest hesitation in asking if they might look at a book, a paper or magazine to see if a particular item is in it before they buy it. On the other hand, there are very few newspapers in one shop in a tiny village that have not already been ordered. Naturally the judge knew this and, having looked at a copy of the previous day's *Daily Mirror* which had been over-ordered, he asked Mrs Buckland if she would be good enough to order a copy of each of the previous day's papers other than the ones he'd looked at.

'I'll get on the telephone at once,' said Mrs Buckland.

'That's very good of you,' said the judge. 'It is rather important and I'd be very grateful.'

'I'm only too pleased to help. Was it something special? An obituary or something?'

'Not exactly,' said the judge.

'Do tell me,' said Mrs Buckland. 'Is it a case of yours? It's very naughty of me, I know, to ask so many questions, but I'm terribly inquisitive. You must have known that for a long time.'

'Oh no,' said the judge gallantly. 'You take a natural interest in local affairs.'

'Nice of you to put it that way.'

'Not at all,' said the judge. He pretended to look round the shop rather than carry on a conversation which was beginning to embarrass him.

'It isn't your picture in the paper, I suppose?' said Mrs Buckland after a moment or two's silence.

'I hope not,' said the judge. 'I mean, no.'

'You're beginning to make it sound very tantalising,' said Mrs Buckland.

The judge threw in his hand.

'It is a photograph I want to see, as a matter of fact,' he said, 'but not one of me.'

'Anyone we know?'

'I don't think so,' said the judge after a moment's pause.

'You mean it might be?'

'You ought to have gone to the Bar,' said the judge. 'You'd have made a very fine cross-examiner.'

'Do tell me who it might be?'

'I don't suppose it is for a moment,' said the judge.

'How funny that you want to see it then.'

'Well, there's no point in being mysterious any more. It might be a photograph of the escaped bank robber, Gladstone.'

'He's in the news again, is he?'

'I don't know that he is, but he might be.'

'But, judge, you rather implied that we might know the man. He hasn't been seen in these parts, has he?'

'I don't think so,' said the judge. And immediately regretted having used the word "think". He knew what would be likely to come. And it came.

'You don't *think* so,' said Mrs Buckland. 'Then who might it be? There've been no strangers round here, as far as I know. Have you seen any?'

'No. Not recently,' said the judge.

'Why, the only newcomer we've had in the last year has been Mr Partridge. I do like him. Don't you?'

'Yes, I do.'

'Has he never told you anything about his wife except that she's abroad?'

'No,' said the judge, 'he hasn't.'

'I find him fascinating,' said Mrs Buckland. 'And he's so kind and generous too. She must be a very lucky woman. I wonder why they don't live together.'

'Well, no one has liked to ask him that,' said the judge. 'It's more the sort of question you'd be likely to ask, if I may say so.'

'I did try, as a matter of fact,' said Mrs Buckland. 'But all I could get from him was that she would be joining him as soon as she could. I wonder what she's like. D'you know – I suppose I oughtn't to say this – but he told me I was one of the most attractive girls he'd ever seen.'

'Well, he's truthful anyway,' said the judge, 'but I hope you won't let it go to your head.'

'I shall behave myself all right,' said Mrs Buckland. 'You can't do anything else in a small community.'

'I agree,' said the judge. 'That's why you don't get crime in close communities. Because everybody knows what everybody else is doing. It's only when you go to the towns where no one knows any one else that crime is at all prevalent. And it's much the same with morals. Morals are always of a high standard in close communities.'

'But you do get husbands running away with other people's wives sometimes in a village,' said Mrs Buckland.

'You do,' said the judge, 'but not very often. It certainly hasn't happened here in my time. Now, how about ringing up to see if you can get hold of those papers? They may be out of stock if we leave it too late.'

'Of course. I'll get on the phone at once.'

The judge had to wait three days for Mrs Buckland to tell him that she'd only been able to get hold of three of the papers he wanted. So there was only one thing to do. He must ring up Bentham.

'I'm so sorry to trouble you, Bentham,' he said, 'but I was a little intrigued at your saying in your letter that you'd seen the photograph of somebody who presumably is rather like my friend Partridge. Could you by any chance tell me which paper it was in?'

'I'm not sure, judge,' said Bentham. 'I saw it in my club and it might have been one of half a dozen.'

'Then would you very much mind telling me who it was a photograph of?'

'It was an actor, as a matter of fact,' said Bentham. 'But for the life of me I can't think of his name. But I can find out for you, judge, if you like.'

'Oh no, that's quite all right,' said the judge. 'I'd have liked to have shown it to Mr Partridge. That was all.'

'I'm so sorry I can't help you more,' said Bentham.

'Not at all,' said the judge. 'And thank you very much for your letter. There's just one other thing before you ring off. Were you by any chance in the Gladstone case? You know – the bank robber who escaped seven or eight months ago.'

'How odd you should ask me that, judge,' said Bentham. 'I wasn't as a matter of fact, but I was going to be and then at the last moment I got "flu" and had to hand the brief on to somebody else.'

'Were you by any chance going to act for Gladstone himself?'

'No, for one of his colleagues.'

'Did you ever see him?'

'Not as far as I remember.'

Bentham would have liked to have asked the judge the reason for his enquiry, but, in view of the rebuff, he had received when he questioned Mr Partridge, he decided to say nothing.

'I'm so sorry to have troubled you,' said the judge, 'and once again thank you very much for your nice letter.'

Well that was plain enough. The judge decided to try to put a stop to the whole ridiculous idea and at the earliest opportunity he tackled the commander about it.

'I want to talk to you about Partridge, George,' he said.

'Have you got his fingerprints at last?'

'You will probably find his fingerprints,' said the judge, 'as a boy on a desk in an institution for orphan children. I hope you feel thoroughly ashamed of yourself. I know that I do.'

'Well, to be quite frank, Bertie,' said the commander, 'I don't. Indeed what you've told me has made me even more suspicious. Did he tell you what he'd been doing for a living?'

'Nothing very definite.'

'I've been looking up this fellow Gladstone,' said the commander. 'D'you know that he was brought up in an institution?'

'Really, this is too bad,' said the judge. 'Is everybody who was brought up in an institution going to be suspected of being a criminal?'

'Of course not,' said the commander. 'But Gladstone escaped. He's still not been caught. They never found the loot. Probably he's got at least several hundred thousand pounds of it himself. Partridge's house must have cost him about twenty thousand. And he's still got to live on something. I don't believe he gave you any idea how he made his money.'

'No, that's perfectly right,' said the judge. 'But he obviously saved.'

'Out of what?' asked the commander. 'If he just went from job to job he couldn't save enough money to put himself in his present position. Château Lafite 1953. Cockburn 1927. And an apparently inexhaustible supply.'

'Well, when it is exhausted,' said the judge, 'we'll certainly be able to claim part of the credit.'

'I suppose he didn't tell you he'd had luck on the pools, by any chance, did he?' asked the commander.

'No, he didn't. He was very embarrassed about it all and I felt very badly about having got it out of him.'

'Now, it's an odd thing,' said the commander. 'I like the fellow. But whether you like a chap or not doesn't depend upon what his morals are. And if he's Gladstone, it's our duty to hand him over.'

'I think your mind's getting warped on the subject. I'm glad you weren't at court with me.'

'Why?'

'Well, one of the counsel appearing in front of me thought he recognised him.'

'Was that counsel by any chance in Gladstone's case?'

'I thought you'd ask that,' said the judge. 'So I found out. He was not.'

'Well, that's purely negative,' said the commander. 'And I really think we ought to do something about it. You don't agree, I gather?'

'I certainly do not,' said the judge. 'I won't agree to anything of which Partridge might learn. His position here or ours or both would become intolerable. One of us might have to leave the neighbourhood.'

'Well, I'm certainly not going to,' said the commander. 'I like it here.'

'So do I,' said the judge. 'And so does Partridge. It would really be too bad when we've accepted the man's hospitality and made him one of ourselves to let it be known to him that some of us suspected him of being an escaped criminal.'

'Would you agree to doing anything of which he didn't learn?'

'Such as?'

'Suppose I go and have a confidential talk with the Chief Constable? That couldn't do any harm.'

The judge considered the suggestion. 'Provided he promises not to do anything that could come to the knowledge of Partridge without our consent, I don't think it would hurt and it might put your mind at rest.'

'But now I come to think of it, I can't make him promise anything like that', said the commander. 'It's his duty to do something about it. How can you go to a policeman and say: "there's a possibility, a very faint possibility, that a man living in the village is really an escaped bank robber", and then tell the policeman that he mustn't do anything about it? He'd have to do something about it.'

'Then I don't agree to your telling the Chief Constable,' said the judge. 'I can't stop you doing it, of course, but I don't think you ought. You've absolutely nothing to go on except your little caricature and the fact that we don't know how he made his money. You must realise that if the police start making enquiries it will reflect on all of us.'

'I shall be quite prepared to take the blame,' said the commander.

'But he knows that we're all friends and that we must have discussed the matter, as we all have. Are you by any chance dining with him next week?'

'As a matter of fact, I am.'

'So am I. Don't you feel a little awkward about doing it, feeling as you do?'

'Not in the least,' said the commander. 'If the fellow's what he says he is – an ordinary respectable citizen – I'm entitled to drink his Château Lafite and his port with the best of them. If he's a crook, why shouldn't I drink it while it lasts? That will be some good he's done in the world. Anyway, if you feel so strongly about it, how is it you're going? You've talked about the possibility of his being Gladstone.'

'That's true,' said the judge. 'As a matter of fact I've done rather more.'

And he told the commander of his telephone conversation with Bentham.

'Well, won't the fillet of sole stick in your throat?' asked the commander.

'I suppose it will a bit,' said the judge.

'I'm surprised at you, Bertie,' said the commander. 'You ought to be more objective. As a judge surely you have to be. I can understand a layman like me worrying about our relationship, but I'm surprised at you. You are trained to be quite dispassionate about everything. You give a man ten years and go out of court and have an excellent lunch without giving a thought to the man's wife or children or anything of that sort.'

'That's not true,' said the judge. 'I do think of them.'

'But it doesn't spoil your lunch,' said the commander. 'That's what I call being objective. Well, at any rate Mary Buckland doesn't know anything about it otherwise the whole village would.'

A Chat in the Shop

'She very nearly did,' said the judge. 'But it's all right, I think.'

'What happened?' asked the commander. The judge told him of his visit to the village store and how he was cross-examined by Mary Buckland.

'She is an attractive girl,' said the commander. 'I suppose it is a bit boring for her in a small place like this with an elderly husband.'

'Middle-aged,' corrected the judge. 'He's about my age. Possibly younger.'

'Sorry,' said the commander. 'Middle-aged. And there's not all that to do. I suppose quite naturally she makes the most of any rumours that happen to be going around.'

'She's very fond of Partridge,' said the judge. 'She'd be horrified to know what we've been saying about him.'

'She'd certainly tell him,' said the commander.

'She would, wouldn't she,' said the judge. 'By jove I was lucky. We'd almost reached the stage when I would have had to admit what it was all about.'

'Are you sure you didn't?' asked the commander.

'I'm pretty certain it's all right,' said the judge. 'As long as she doesn't put two and two together. Well, there's nothing I can do about it anyway. We must hope for the best.'

'Elizabeth won't hear a word against him,' said the commander.

'You've talked it over with her, have you?' asked the judge.

'Of course I have,' said the commander. 'Haven't you talked it over with Betty?'

'She thinks he may have had wife trouble. He's certainly very vague about what's happened to his wife. Betty thinks there may have been a scandal which he doesn't want raked up.'

'Possible I suppose,' said the commander, 'but not very convincing to me.' He paused for a moment and then added: 'I wonder what he does all day.'

At that moment Mr Partridge was in fact chatting in the village store to Mrs Buckland.

'Can you keep a secret?' he said.

'As well as most women.'

'Well, I knew that,' said Mr Partridge. 'But will you keep this especially all to yourself?'

'Is it very exciting?'

'It is for me.'

'Will other people be excited?'

'I hope some of them will.'

'Will I be excited?'

'You'll be interested.'

'Why won't I be excited if other people may be?'

'Will you keep it to yourself? Not for long. Everybody will know within a week.'

'All right. I will for you. I don't believe I would for anybody else.'

'Not even for your husband?'

'Well, that's different. Husbands don't count.'

'D'you mean that?' said Mr Partridge looking her full in the face.

'No, I don't.'

'Pity,' said Mr Partridge. 'It is, isn't it?'

'To tell you the truth, I'd like to be bad sometimes, but it really wouldn't be worth it.'

'How right you are,' said Mr Partridge. 'But how few young women of your age recognise it.'

'Well, what's the secret?'

At that moment Mrs Blinkhorn came in. 'Hullo, Mr Partridge,' she said, 'how nice to see you here.'

'Do call me Donald,' he said, 'before you dine with me next week.'

'How nice of you. Of course I will. And you'll do the same with me. Do go on serving him first, Mary. Don't mind me. I'll just look around.'

'I've finished, as a matter of fact,' said Mr Partridge. 'There's only one further thing I want and I don't want you to know what it is. I want to keep it secret until you dine with me next week.'

'How exciting.' said Mrs Blinkhorn.

'I hope it will come up to expectation,' said Mr Partridge, 'but you can never be sure. Expectation is so often much more pleasant than realisation.'

'Well, I don't find it so,' said Mrs Blinkhorn. 'Do you, Mary?'

'Very occasionally,' said Mrs Buckland. Eventually the commander's wife gave her order and, after a few more words with Mr Partridge she left.

'Oh, thank God,' said Mrs Buckland. 'How tantalising. Now tell me.'

'After all this build-up.' said Mr Partridge, 'I'm afraid you may be very disappointed, but next Thursday when I'm giving this dinner party is a very special occasion.'

'Have you been knighted or something?'

'Nothing like that. But my wife's coming back.'

'Oh, how lovely,' said Mrs Buckland.

'Well, she is,' said Mr Partridge, 'and I'm like a small boy waiting for presents on Christmas Day. I can hardly sleep for thinking of it.'

'How long has she been away?'

'About six months.'

'I rather thought you were separated.'

'Good gracious no. Not in the way that you mean. She's half French and her mother died recently and she had to go and wind up her affairs.'

'Why didn't you go with her?'

'That's a point,' said Mr Partridge. 'The truth of the matter is that I wanted to get this place warmed up ready for her to come to. I wanted to get to know people first so that she could really call it home when she arrived. Everybody's been extremely nice to me and I'm sure they'll like her. But I thought I'd pave the way.'

'When is she actually coming?'

'Not till Wednesday, as a matter of fact.'

'Will she like a dinner party as soon after she gets back?'

'I thought of that but I'm being selfish, I'm afraid. I want to show her off. I shouldn't say this, I suppose, but she's as attractive as you.'

'Thank you. Aren't you frightened of her meeting some handsome stranger while she's in France?'

'Not really,' said Mr Partridge. 'I don't think it could happen, but if it could it would be because she wanted to and if she wanted it I'd accept it.'

'Wouldn't you be in the least bit jealous?'

'Jealous? No,' said Mr Partridge. 'Disappointed perhaps and certainly I'd be unhappy for a time. It's a funny thing, you know. I'd be absolutely brokenhearted if I lost her – I mean if she were killed or died or something – but if she went off with another man I certainly wouldn't be brokenhearted. We've all got a certain amount of pride, I suppose, and it might give that a jolt but I shouldn't go about with my head in a sling.'

'You're too conceited, that's the matter with you,' said Mrs Buckland. 'You know perfectly well she'd never go off with anyone else, you're so confident about that that when you talk of her doing so you are not talking about a real possibility.'

'Perhaps you're right,' said Mr Partridge. 'I do feel sure that she'll come back and it's also true, I suppose, that no one can tell what he will do in a particular circumstance unless that circumstance arises.'

'Why do you want to keep it so secret?' asked Mrs Buckland.

'Only because I want to give them a surprise. It's the child in me, I suppose. But she really will take their breath away when they see her.'

'But you'd get that effect provided they'd never seen her until the dinner party.'

'Well, it would be very difficult sometimes. Some of them might come snooping around to have a preview, as it were. And another thing. I'm not quite a fool, you know, and I know the way people talk about me. Is he married or isn't he? Are they separated? Is there a divorce? Or what? No, I want suddenly to produce her and I'll eat my hat if it isn't a knock-out.'

'What's she like otherwise?'

'Well, I'm prejudiced, of course, but she's a sensible girl. Quite a sense of humour. She's got a lot of interests. I'll tell you one thing about her. She's as good a listener as she is a talker. There are very few people you can say that about. Certainly not about me.'

They went on talking for some time and, before they'd finished, the estate manager, Brian Hudson, came in.

'Someone told me you were leaving us,' he said to Mr Partridge.

'Who was that?'

'Oh, I don't know. I thought I'd heard someone say that you were going. Just one of those rumours, you know.'

'Without the slightest foundation,' said Mr Partridge.

'Good,' said Mr Hudson. 'I hate changes. It usually gives me extra work and I like to keep the faces I know about the place. I'll carry those in for you, Mary,' he said, as he saw Mrs Buckland trying to carry in a crate of bottles.

'Oh, how kind,' said Mrs Buckland. Mr Hudson picked up the crate of bottles as though they weighed only a couple of pounds.

'Good gracious,' said Mr Partridge. 'Are you a weightlifter?'

'Well I have tried it but it's rather boring. I don't really care for it. Boxing used to be my line. Only in an amateur way, you know.'

'I love boxing,' said Mrs Buckland. 'I shouldn't, I know. But I'm all animal when I see those marvellous bodies in the ring.'

'Shall I strip for you now?' asked Mr Hudson.

CHAPTER TEN

The Informer

While the judge was talking to the commander about Mr Partridge and while Mr Partridge was talking to Mrs Buckland, Chief Superintendent Beales was interviewing Geoffrey Wentworth.

'They tell me,' said the superintendent, 'that you can tell us where Gladstone is.'

'Straight and to the point,' said Mr Wentworth. 'Too much to the point for my liking.'

'What on earth d'you mean by that?'

'I like to play around a bit, you know. You're a married man, I take it, so you know what I mean. If you just say: "Where's Gladstone?" and I say: "Timbuctoo" and you say: "Here's £25 for your trouble" it would be over in a couple of minutes.'

'Well, I'm a busy man,' said the superintendent.

'I'm not. I've all the time in the world. And it's at your disposal.'

'If it hadn't been reported to me by two of my subordinates that they believed that you really had worthwhile information, I should kick you out,' said the superintendent.

'Kick away,' said Mr Wentworth. 'If you actually kick me it will cost you £5 a kick, if it does no permanent damage.

If you mean that you just want me to go, I'll go quietly of course and that will mean that you don't find Mr Gladstone. Not as a result of this visit anyway. You may find him on your own of course, but I doubt it. Not just yet anyway. People who use fire engines and ambulances need a lot of coppers to catch them and coppers with brains too. I take it you're one of the few with brains.'

'I don't propose to discuss the subject,' said the superintendent.

'Well I do,' said Mr Wentworth. 'We play this game my way or not at all. How long have you been in the Force?'

The superintendent got up. 'I'll be back shortly,' he said, and left the room. He went straight to an assistant commissioner.

'Look, sir,' he said, 'this chap's just being bloody insulting. Have I got to stand for it?'

'Use your own judgment, chief,' said the assistant commissioner. 'I'm told that this man really can lead us to him. If you're satisfied that I'm wrong, get rid of him by all means. D'you think it's just a hoax?'

'I haven't the faintest idea,' said the superintendent. 'He hasn't told me a thing yet. He's simply trying to make me angry.'

'He seems to have succeeded,' said the assistant commissioner.

'He has,' said the superintendent. 'If we didn't want Gladstone so badly, I'd have hoofed him out without coming to see you.'

'Why have you come to see me?'

'Just to let off steam.'

'You know as well as I do that we've completely lost the man for the moment. The police have been made to look blithering idiots. We couldn't even move him from the Old Bailey to Brixton and later when we had completely cornered him we let him drive calmly out in an ambulance. So personally I'd stand a great many insults if I thought the man insulting me could really give me some information.'

'You're quite right, sir,' said the superintendent. 'I'll go back and humble myself.'

'You should enjoy it,' said the assistant commissioner. 'It'll be a new experience. I mean that. Play it his way. Have some fun. I don't suppose you've anything else to do this morning.'

'Nothing else to – ' began the superintendent.

'Sorry, chief,' said the assistant commissioner. 'It's not fair for me to pull your leg as well.'

The superintendent went back to Mr Wentworth. 'Right,' he said, 'now we can get down to business. First of all, would you care for a drink?'

'That's very civil,' said Mr Wentworth. 'But I never drink while I'm working.'

'Well,' said the superintendent, 'if you don't mind, I do.' He opened a cupboard disclosing a bottle of whisky and a syphon and poured himself a whisky and soda. 'Here's fun,' he said. 'That's what you've come for, I gather.'

'I was asking you, superintendent, how long you'd been in the Police Force?'

'Twenty-five years.'

'You're now a chief superintendent. Likely to go any further?'

'Not before I die,' said the superintendent.

'So this is your ceiling?'

'Too true.'

'How old are you?'

'Fifty-three,' said the superintendent.

'A bit long in the tooth for the rough and tumble?'

'I could still give a good account of myself if necessary.'

'I'm sure you could. You're giving quite a good account now. Shall we get down to business?'

'Any time you like,' said the superintendent. 'I'm entirely in your hands. Your very capable hands, if I may say so.'

'We'll see how capable they are at the end of this interview, superintendent. I can see that I've met my match. I thought I hadn't, but I congratulate you.'

'Not at all,' said the superintendent. 'I'm grateful to you for the lesson. Was there something else I could tell you about myself? As you've surmised, I'm married. Three children. Hobby, gardening when I've got time?'

'How about chess?' said Mr Wentworth.

'Yes,' said the superintendent. 'I do that a bit too.'

'D'you do problems at all?'

'Sometimes.'

'Two-movers or three-movers?'

'I can do two-movers,' said the superintendent, 'but three-movers usually have me beat.'

'A lot of people say they can play chess,' said Mr Wentworth, 'but they can't. A lot of people try to solve problems but they can't. D'you know how to tell if a person has no idea at all about problems? Here you are. White to play and mate in two moves. If the person trying to solve the problem tries one particular move, that shows he doesn't know the first thing about problem solving. What is that particular move?'

'Putting the other side in check,' said the superintendent.

'My God!' said Mr Wentworth. 'If I had a hat I'd take it off to you. You know what you're talking about.'

'Sometimes,' said the superintendent. 'And I gather you know what you're talking about, Mr Wentworth.'

'Sometimes,' said Mr Wentworth.

'Is this one of those times?' asked the superintendent.

112

'That's what I'm here to find out,' said Mr Wentworth. 'Inflation's terrible, don't you think?'

'Terrible,' agreed the superintendent.

'You buy information, don't you?' asked Mr Wentworth.

'Sometimes,' said the superintendent.

'Well, as it's your staple diet,' said Mr Wentworth, 'sometimes must be pretty often.'

'We don't always *pay*,' said the superintendent. 'Not in money anyway.'

'But I take it that you intend to pay this time?'

'Certainly,' said the superintendent, 'if we can get what we want. What sort of figure had you in mind?' he added.

'Now, now, superintendent,' said Mr Wentworth, 'you're going too fast.'

'Silly of me,' said the superintendent. 'I apologise.'

'I like to explore the situation first,' said Mr Wentworth, 'but I should make it plain straight away that I can't promise the return of any money. Would I be right in thinking that if the sum required for information is more than you were prepared to pay out of police funds, the bank would be prepared to assist?'

'It's possible,' said the superintendent. 'Obviously it depends on what the information is.'

'Information likely to lead to the arrest of Gladstone. Even if he hasn't the money on him, the bank surely wants him behind bars as an example to others.'

'Yes,' said the superintendent. 'I think they'd probably help.'

'Well, I'd better tell you my terms,' said Mr Wentworth. 'You've been very patient and you deserve a break.'

'That's very good of you,' said the superintendent. 'I don't want a penny for what I tell you if it does not turn out to be accurate. I want five thousand pounds if it does and I want twenty thousand pounds if it leads to

Gladstone's arrest. And I'm not prepared to bargain about the figure.'

'I'd have to take instructions, of course,' said the superintendent. 'I gather you're not open to an offer.'

'Definitely not,' said Mr Wentworth. 'But equally I don't expect you to buy a pig in a poke. Before you agree to pay anything you obviously must know the nature of the information.'

'We should certainly be very grateful for that,' said the superintendent.

'Well,' said Mr Wentworth. 'I can tell you where Gladstone was seven months ago and I can tell you where he has a house now, but I don't guarantee that that information will lead to his arrest. The lack of the guarantee, superintendent, is possibly due to the fact that even when you've got Mr Gladstone you don't seem to be able to keep him. And if you know where he is, you don't seem to be able to arrest him. That won't be my fault if the information that I give you is correct. Now, what do you say? Oh I should have said that there's a further piece of information that I can give you which will be very useful but I'm not prepared to disclose that at this stage until we come to terms.'

'Can I ask you a question?' said the superintendent.

'Certainly,' said Mr Wentworth.

'You may not want to answer it,' said the superintendent.

'Then I won't,' said Mr Wentworth.

'Will you please understand that I'm not intending to be offensive when I ask it.'

'If you'd said that ten minutes ago, superintendent, I wouldn't have believed it. But your present attitude shows that the last thing in the world you want to be to me is offensive. What is the question?'

'Well, Mr Wentworth,' said the superintendent, 'whether Mr Gladstone has the whole of the two and a half million pounds or not of course we don't know, but no doubt he has a very large portion of it. He's therefore in a position to pay you much more for not coming to us than we are for giving him away. Why do you come to us?'

'Take care of the pence,' said Mr Wentworth, 'and the pounds will take care of themselves. The twenty thousand pounds I'm asking from you is chicken feed. But chicken feed feeds chickens and I don't despise it.'

'You mean you have been to ask him?' asked the superintendent. 'No, I'm sorry, I shouldn't have asked that.'

'I don't mind your asking it,' said Mr Wentworth. 'I'm an enquiry agent of a sort, you know. My job is to get information for people and to withhold information from people. Some people pay me to withhold it. Other people pay me to get it. If you pay me, you'll be paying me to get it. If Mr Gladstone paid me, he'd be paying me to withhold it. It's quite simple, you see. It stinks a bit, doesn't it? Rather like an agent who takes commission from both sides. And that's illegal, isn't it? But I manage to keep on the right side of the law.'

'Very proper,' said the superintendent. 'Well, I'll have to make a report about this. You can tell us where Gladstone was seven months ago and where he now has a house and you can also give us a useful piece of information which will help to his arrest.'

'Exactly.'

'And you want five thousand pounds if it's proved that he was where you say seven months ago and that he has got the house which you say he now has.'

'Correct.'

'And if he's arrested as a result of that information, and of the other information you say you can give us, then you want a total of twenty thousand pounds.'

'If I said total,' said Mr Wentworth, 'that was a slip. I want a further twenty thousand pounds. Twenty-five thousand pounds in all on his arrest. Well now, what do you say?'

'I must take instructions.'

'How long will that take?'

'Two or three days. I don't think we've your address.'

'No you haven't.'

'Or your telephone number?'

'I usually use a callbox.'

'Any particular callbox?'

'Sometimes. But I shan't call you. I'll come here. At eleven o'clock, shall we say, on Friday? All right, superintendent?' The superintendent nodded assent. 'Then I look forward to seeing you again at eleven o'clock on Friday. Just one other thing, superintendent,' said Mr Wentworth as he rose to go. 'Don't have me tailed. It wouldn't do any good. On the contrary. I'll double the price if you do.'

'All right,' said the superintendent. 'I won't.'

'You were going to, of course,' said Mr Wentworth. 'You'd better call them off.'

'Very well,' said the superintendent. 'It shall be as you wish.'

Mr Wentworth left Scotland Yard and did not bother to look back to see whether he was being followed. It would not be worth their while.

Punctually at eleven o'clock on the following Friday he called to see the superintendent. After a few preliminary civilities the superintendent said, 'Your terms are acceptable, Mr Wentworth. Provided the information is definite and correct.'

'You must have had a good report about me,' said Mr Wentworth. 'I never thought you'd agree. To be quite frank, I'd have taken half of that.'

'You said you wouldn't bargain about it,' said the superintendent.

'Of course I did,' said Mr Wentworth. 'What d'you take me for? If I'd shown in any way that I was open to an offer you would have made me one. All the same, I'm a little surprised that you didn't try it on. You must be sure that I've got the goods.'

'You won't get anything if you haven't got them.'

'True enough. You people don't make offers like that unless you mean business and think that I mean it too. Well, I do as a matter of fact. I want that money put in the joint names of my solicitors and anyone on your behalf you like.'

'Hang it,' said the superintendent. 'We're good for the money. You could sue us if we didn't pay.'

'I wouldn't want the publicity.'

'Is it because you don't trust us? Because if that's so, putting it in joint names won't be any better for you. We can always refuse to give a release.'

'You're less likely to do that if the money is there,' said Mr Wentworth, 'if it's actually in the bank. If it's a question of finding twenty-five thousand pounds or even five thousand pounds, for that matter, all sorts of difficulties arise. The gentleman who could sign the cheque isn't there and so on. But if the money's in the bank awaiting release on one signature, the transaction is an easier one from my point of view.'

'Who are your solicitors then?'

'I'll have to find some,' said Mr Wentworth.

'They'll want your name and address, you know,' said the superintendent.

'They won't be able to give it away,' said Mr Wentworth. 'And anyway I can always change it. I often do.'

'Really?' said the superintendent. 'For health reasons, I suppose.'

'Sometimes. Well now, here's the information. Have you got your machine working?'

'Machine?' queried the superintendent, a little too innocently.

'You're taping this, of course,' said Mr Wentworth.

'I was forgetting,' said the superintendent lamely.

'Well,' said Mr Wentworth, 'seven months ago Gladstone was in the Argentine in a place called Realico where he stayed at an hotel with an English name. It's called "The Fortune". Most appropriate, don't you think? He then went to the South of France where he rented a house in a little village called St Monat. The address of the house is 9, rue Labiche and he's still paying the rent.'

'And does he live there?' asked the superintendent.

'No. He hasn't been living there for the last six months.'

'Where's he gone?'

'I've no idea. But,' said Mr Wentworth, 'this is information which is worth all of five thousand pounds, I should have thought – *but* his wife is still living there. If you tail her she'll lead you to him.'

'If that's true,' said the superintendent. 'You shall have your five thousand pounds as soon as we've confirmed it is true.'

Shortly afterwards Mr Wentworth left the superintendent and walked away from Scotland Yard. He was quite pleased with himself. If charm and a sense of humour are virtues those were the only virtues possessed by Mr Wentworth. Early in his career as an accountant he had decided that honest living was not for him. He was a very similar man to Gladstone himself, completely antisocial, completely selfish and with a profound dislike of regular work. But the sort of adventures that Gladstone organised did not appeal to him either. Robbing banks or holding up railway trains were not the way he proposed to earn his living. His weapons were his brains and his tongue and he made a very good living out of blackmailing criminals and informing the police. But he was careful never to mix up the two. He knew that if he took money from a criminal for keeping quiet about something and then told the police, he would live in permanent danger of death or injury. So he would not have dreamed of extracting money from Gladstone, as the superintendent had suggested, for keeping quiet about his whereabouts and at the same time giving information to the police about him. He had no objection to letting the superintendent think that he did both. He realised that he might not get his twenty-five thousand pounds, for Gladstone would not easily be caught. But five thousand pounds for a couple of interviews with Scotland Yard was satisfactory remuneration if one bears in mind that he had only obtained by accident the information which he was prepared to sell. Had he had to pay a sufficiently substantial sum for it naturally he would have charged the superintendent more. Then he suddenly remembered something. He telephoned Scotland Yard and spoke to the superintendent.

'Oh, superintendent,' he said, 'there's one thing you didn't ask me and I forgot to tell you. In France he uses the name André Savoir and he took the house in that name.'

'How shall we know it's the same man?' asked the superintendent.

'Take a photograph with you,' said Wentworth patiently. 'Show it to the milkman in St Monat, to the baker and the rest of them. They will recognise him all right. And, when that's done, I want my five thousand pounds.'

'You shall have it,' said the superintendent. He, too, was pleased. The banks generally had taken the escape of Gladstone very seriously indeed and had offered to pay up to a hundred thousand pounds for his recapture.

CHAPTER ELEVEN

Mrs Partridge

The commander and the judge had just finished a game of croquet. It had been a very close finish and they were therefore very pleased.

'Here you are,' said the judge, handing over fifty pence. 'Money well spent.'

'Thank you,' said the commander. 'It was a good game, I thought you were going to win.'

'I should have if I hadn't missed that last shot,' said the judge. 'I think we're improving you know.'

'You always say that when it's a close thing,' said the commander. 'The truth is that we're just about as bad as each other. Partridge, who's obviously never played the game before, will beat either of us in a few months.'

'Partridge,' said the commander. 'I keep on thinking about him, you know. I can't help it. One thing I've noticed. He doesn't seem to have any friends – I mean apart from those in the neighbourhood. You never see any strange cars outside his house and when I'm in the garden I never hear strange voices over the wall. I wonder what letters he has. If Mary dealt with the post we might learn something from her.'

'That's quite disgraceful, George,' said the judge. 'I'm quite sure you wouldn't. Mary's a very trustworthy girl.'

'If only the telephones weren't automatic these days, we might have found out something from the exchange. In the old days when the telephone went through the local post office the postmaster or postmistress was a mine of information. You didn't have to ask, they told you. But why doesn't he have any friends?'

'You're dining with him on Thursday, aren't you? What d'you call yourself?'

'Close friends, I mean. Or acquaintances other than those round here.'

'It's possible,' said the judge, 'that he's blotted his copybook some time and even gone to prison, changed his name and come to a new neighbourhood and is trying to forget the past.'

'Or even have escaped from prison,' put in the commander.

'Yes, that's possible,' said the judge, 'but we've had all this out before. I don't know why it still rankles with you. He's an excellent neighbour, he gives no trouble of any kind to anyone and is always ready to help if any help is required in any direction and perhaps, most important of all, he's improving at croquet. You mark my words, he'll be giving us bisques before we've finished.'

'But he's no wife, no girlfriend, nothing. It doesn't make sense for an educated man.'

'Supposing he was a stockbroker and was hammered and got some years for some kind of conversion. He does his seven years and then he wants to start afresh and while he's in prison his wife dies and he's got no near relatives. As a matter of fact, my stockbroker went bust about ten years ago and got three years. It's the sort of thing he might have done. A lot of people are very vain, you know. They like to be thought "all right". If a chap comes out of prison after a long sentence and he goes back to live in his original neighbourhood and under his original name he must know perfectly well that, as he walks in the street even in the village, somebody will be saying to some stranger: "D'you know who that is? That's Horatio Bottomley." "Good gracious, I didn't know he lived here," says the stranger. I'm afraid that's how most people behave. Well, you'd do it yourself. If you had a friend down for the day and you passed a man who'd done seven years – of course you'd wait till you were well out of earshot and then you'd say; "Who'd you think that was? Leopold Harris." It takes a lot of courage to live with that sort of thing. Some people can't avoid it, of course, because they have too many acquaintances all over the place and there's practically nowhere they could go without being recognised by somebody. Some people are too proud in a way to run away from it. If I'd been disbarred and sent to prison – by the way I can only think of one barrister who has in the last fifty years, but I expect there've been one or two more – but if that happened to me I don't think I would have wanted to go back to my old home town. Even if people got used to seeing you and you got used to seeing them the conversation would always be an embarrassment. There would be words that couldn't be used at all. Prison could never be mentioned. Courts could never be mentioned. The crime wave couldn't be talked about or reformation of the criminal and the sentencing powers of the courts and so on. Oh no, I can well understand a man who'd done something of that sort wanting to get away from it all. Cutting all his previous connections and starting absolutely afresh.'

'That would account for everything,' said the commander, 'except my little drawing. I look at it sometimes. It is really very like him, you know.'

'My dear George,' said the judge, 'try drawing his beard on another face and you'll find that's very like him too. You see, you've copied his beard and moustache and that gives the outline of the man you know. Although every head is different many people have similar sorts of heads. There's nothing special about Partridge's, nor Gladstone's. So you look up a few photographs of people with similar type heads and put your moustache and beard on them and you will find they look like Partridge.'

'All you say is very true, Bertie,' said the commander, 'but I have a sort of intuitive feeling about the matter. You must have had one sometimes in cases.'

'On the occasions when I do,' said the judge, 'I ignore it. I try cases on the evidence, on the probabilities and/or on the argument, not upon hunches. Sometimes when I've been trying a case it's been disclosed at an early stage that there's a man going to give evidence and there are a lot of allegations against him, rather nasty allegations. When I used to look round the court I'd say to myself, "That's the fellow". As often as not I was wrong. The man I'd chosen as a villain would be a highly respectable solicitor or architect or doctor or something of that sort. But there are a few judges who think they can see into the hearts of men. "I think I usually know when a person's speaking the truth," they say. If they do, they're better men than I am. In seventy-five per cent of cases the truth comes out fairly easily and there's no necessity for hunches or intuitive feelings. In another fifteen per cent it is not so easy, but if you pay attention to the whole circumstances of the case and judge by the probabilities in the majority of cases you get the right result. In the remaining ten per cent, it is very difficult indeed to prise open the truth and there are few good judges who in those cases feel certain they've arrived at the right conclusion as far as the facts are concerned. So give up your hunches, George, and enjoy his claret and port while they last.'

'I'll do that,' said the commander. 'Indeed, I'm looking forward to next Thursday.'

It was certainly a big night at Mr Partridge's house on the following Thursday. He had invited the whole neighbourhood and they all came. They were all talking and drinking happily when Mr Partridge asked for silence for a moment and turned on the wireless.

'I believe there's some news about that bank robber,' he said. 'Someone told me there'd been a news flash and that it was to be repeated in the news.'

Mr Partridge was right. After a few other items the announcer said, 'A spokesman from Scotland Yard has stated that the Yard are convinced that they know where Gladstone is at present but, apart from stating that he is somewhere in one of the South American republics they are not prepared to disclose any further information at the moment, except that it is a republic with whom we have an extradition treaty and that an arrest is expected imminently.'

The superintendent had given out the item quite deliberately in order not to let Gladstone think that they were really on his track.

'Well, that doesn't get them much further,' said Mr Partridge. 'South America is a big place. If he's in Chile, he'll go to Peru. If he's in Peru, he'll go to Chile.'

'But no doubt people will be watching the house where he is,' said the judge.

'They've done that before, haven't they,' said Mr Partridge. 'I think it's very stupid of them to give a man like Gladstone any information at all as to their knowledge. Of course it may simply be a rumour and be false or it might be deliberately false. A blind to make him think he's safe, when they really know that he's somewhere else. They do that sort of thing. I don't blame them. I'd do it myself. Ah, here's the vicar. That's the lot, I think.'

When he'd satisfied himself that all his guests were there, Mr Partridge held up his hand.

'I've asked you here tonight,' he said, 'for a very special reason. My wife and I are reunited. Here she is.'

As he spoke, the door opened and his wife came in. He had not exaggerated her beauty. There were murmurs of admiration all round the room. Mr Partridge took his wife and introduced her one by one to all the company.

'I'm going to put you between the judge and the commander,' he said, just before they went in to dinner. The two men were extremely pleased. Mrs Partridge was not only attractive and beautiful but she was superbly dressed and her smile was one to be remembered.

'Are you a kindly man?' she asked the judge.

'I'm normal, I suppose.'

'In court, I mean,' said Mrs Partridge. 'D'you make your witnesses feel at home or that at any moment they may be cast out into utter darkness?'

'Well,' said the judge, 'you should come with me some time and see. It's very difficult to form an objective view of one's own behaviour. I'd be delighted to take you. Sit on the bench with me and judge for yourself.'

'That would be most exciting.'

'Your husband should be able to tell you something about it because he came to court with me one day. The only trouble about your sitting on the bench, if I may say so, is that everyone in court would be looking at you instead of me and you might attract counsel's attention too much.' The judge paused for a moment.

'Go on,' said Mrs Partridge, 'I love it.'

'In that case,' said the commander, 'while the judge is getting his second wind – I think you are the most beautiful woman I've ever seen in Little Bacon.'

'A population of seventy-five?' enquired Mrs Partridge.

'How stupid of me,' said the commander, 'I should have said anywhere. In London. In England. In the world.'

'How many wives in how many ports do sailors keep these days?' asked Mrs Partridge.

'I've retired,' said the commander. 'And I had to sign the Official Secrets Act, so I'm not allowed to tell you.'

'D'you find it difficult to be a sailor in peacetime, commander?' asked Mrs Partridge.

'I told you. I'm retired.'

'Yes, but before you retired. I mean if you're a doctor you cut people up. If you're a lawyer you argue cases. If you're an accountant you add up figures and so on. And all of it is what you've been trained for. But soldiers and sailors are brought up to kill. They are not allowed to do that in peacetime. How did you manage?'

'We trained and had exercises.'

'But how boring. A surgeon wouldn't have much fun cutting up a dummy, or an architect playing with children's bricks.'

'Well, someone's got to do the job.'

'Of course, and I for one am most grateful to you for doing it, but I just wondered if you ever hankered after a bloody battle.'

'I certainly didn't. You're right in saying that soldiers and sailors have the job of killing. True enough, but they also have the job of being killed. You can't do one without the other and I'd willingly forego the pleasure of killing to avoid the risk of being killed.'

'My husband was a soldier once,' she said, lowering her voice. 'But only in the war, you know. He got decorated twice, but don't let him know that I told you. He's rather shy about it.'

'What was his regiment?' asked the judge.

'He was a gunner, as a matter of fact. So were you, weren't you, judge?'

'How did you know?'

'Oh, I did my homework. You don't put much in *Who's Who* about yourself, but I read what little you did put. You didn't put any hobbies.'

'I haven't any really,' said the judge. 'And anyway I don't see why I should make them public. Have you any hobbies?'

'If it's a hobby,' said Mrs Partridge, 'I love talking to intelligent men.'

'As for that,' said the commander, 'I love talking to beautiful women. What would you say your husband's hobbies were?'

'Wine and crime. When I say "crime", I don't mean he goes out burgling in the evenings but he's interested in the people who do.'

'Yes, of course,' said the judge. 'He put on the wireless just before you came in to hear an announcement about the escaped bank robber Gladstone.'

'I'm certainly interested in him,' said the commander.

'Most people find there's something rather glamorous about a man who escapes from prison,' said the judge. 'I confess I don't share their views. For one thing, he may commit more crimes. For another, I've a strong objection to his being able to enjoy the loot.'

'I couldn't help overhearing that,' said Partridge. 'No, I agree with you in one way. On the other hand, think what it must be like wondering when the blow's going to fall. That can't be much fun. I expect some days he wishes he were back safely in jail.'

'One of the earlier reports,' said the commander, 'said that he had been seen with a beautiful girl in Brazil. At least he can enjoy himself until the blow falls.'

'If the girl's his wife,' said Mr Partridge, 'it must be worse for her.'

'Oh I don't suppose it's his wife,' said the commander.

'Why not?' asked Mrs Partridge. 'Aren't wives ever beautiful.'

'I don't mean that. Criminals always seem to have molls or whatever you call them.'

'Well, if I were on the run,' said Partridge, 'I'd be happier with my wife whatever she looked like.'

'And if I were on the run,' said the judge, 'I'd as soon be on the run with Mrs Partridge as anyone else – apart from my wife, of course.'

'I've just been rereading Galsworthy's *Escape*,' said the commander. 'D'you remember that in that the parson conceals an escaped convict. Would you, Harvey?'

'I doubt it,' said the vicar. 'It depends on all the circumstances.'

'But if you believed the man was innocent?' asked Mr Partridge.

'That would be different,' said the vicar.

'It shouldn't be,' said the judge. 'If you believe a man innocent, by all means take every possible step to have his innocence established and his guilt wiped out. But as long as he's a convicted man you ought to hand him over.'

'But judge, suppose you knew he was innocent?' asked Mr Partridge.

'You can't know a man is innocent,' said the judge, 'unless you've committed the crime yourself and you knew that he had nothing to do with it. People are always using the word "know" when they really mean "believe". When I was a barrister I was often asked: "What do you do when you know your client is guilty?" Well, you can only know he's guilty if either he tells you he's guilty or if you've seen him commit the crime. If you've seen him commit the crime you couldn't appear for him at all because you'd be a witness. If it's because he's told you that he's guilty, although you could appear for him you could only appear for him to this extent that you'd be entitled to see if the prosecution proved its case. You couldn't suggest, for example, that he was elsewhere at the time of the crime or put him in the witness box to tell lies.'

'But if you believe your client is guilty,' said Mrs Partridge, 'I mean really conscientiously believe him to be guilty – can you properly appear for him?'

'Most certainly,' said the judge. 'For one thing, your belief might be incorrect and, if it were and you refused to appear, so might every other barrister. In other words, he wouldn't be able to find anyone to defend him but every barrister would be trying him in private in his own chambers. In fact the man's entitled to a trial by a jury before a judge.'

'I quite understand that,' said Mrs Partridge, 'but surely it must affect your confidence in your case if you don't believe it.'

'Not in the least,' said the judge. 'Professional advocates shouldn't mind one way or the other. Their duty is simply to do the best they can for their clients. Lawyers have to try to be objective.'

'Are you objective, judge?' said Mrs Partridge.

'In court, yes,' said the judge.

'But warm hearted and lovable outside.'

'I should like to think so.'

'And so should I,' said Mrs Partridge.

'Well,' said the commander, 'I'm warm hearted and lovable all the time.'

'Aren't I lucky?' said Mrs Partridge. 'And I've got a husband who's more warm hearted and lovable than all of you put together.'

'I couldn't help hearing that remark,' said Mr Partridge.

'You were intended to, darling.'

Whether or not Mrs Partridge was the most beautiful woman ever to be seen in Little Bacon it is highly probable that the dinner was the best that had ever been eaten there. Mr Partridge had really set out to please his guests, and even had alternative dishes for some of the courses. He knew, for example, that Mrs Winchcombe didn't like oysters and that the judge and commander liked them immensely. The evening was a huge success and when it was over, the commander again asked the judge if he might walk home with him.

'Well, what is it this time, George? Don't you think she's lovely.'

'Marvellous,' said the commander. 'She might have been the girl he was seen with in Brazil.'

'For heaven's sake!' said the judge. 'Your obsession's getting the better of you.'

'Well, that's why I wanted to walk home with you, Bertie,' said the commander. 'It is. And I've got to do something about it and I'm going to and I thought I'd tell you. I daresay you won't approve. You may even tell me not to, but I'm going to do it just the same.'

'You're going to the police?'

'Not just like that,' said the commander. 'I quite agree that if I simply went to them and suggested that they should have a look at him that might be too embarrassing. So what I am going to do is to take his fingerprints surreptitiously. Yes, surreptitiously. It does go against the grain a bit, but it won't do anybody any harm and you're the only person who will know besides me.'

'You mean on a glass or a plate or something of that sort.'

'That's right,' said the commander. 'Then I shall take it down to the police and ask them to have it examined. If the examination clears him nobody will know anything about it and no harm will be done, and if my feelings turn out to be right then we shall have got him.'

'They're feelings now, are they?' said the judge.

'Strong feelings?'

'It's no good trying to cross-examine me, Bertie. The thing is getting me down and I'm going to bring it to an end. I was talking to the vicar the other day and he said – '

'So he's in it too,' said the judge.

'We're all in it in a way,' said the commander. 'They're none of us who haven't talked about it at some time. You can't help it.'

'What about Mary Buckland?' asked the judge. 'Have you told her your suspicions?'

'No, I haven't, as a matter of fact. She likes him too much. It might hurt her feelings.'

'When are you going to do this?'

'Well, I shall give a drinks party next week and invite him.'

'I suppose the invitations won't read, "You are invited to a fingerprint party"?'

'All right,' said the commander. 'I know it's a very unpleasant thing to do, but I'm going to do it. As a matter of fact, I think probably we've all got a duty to do it. I shan't tell the police whose fingerprints they are, unless they turn out to be Gladstone's. In which case you'll be as glad as I shall be that I tried it on.'

'I'm not surprised that they gave you a DSC,' said the judge. 'It takes more guts than I've got to do anything like this. Will Elizabeth know about it?'

'Yes, she'll have to, otherwise we might make a mess of it.'

'And you'll say: "How are you, Partridge, my dear fellow. So glad you were able to come. What will you have?" '

'Yes, I shall do all that. I shall give him a drink in a glass specially polished to take his fingerprints. I shall then pretend to find something wrong with the drink I've given him, take the glass away and give him another drink. I shall then excuse myself, carefully wrap the glass up in a handkerchief and put it away until after the party. Then I shall go straight down to the police station. You ought to be grateful to me really, because I believe that secretly you're worrying almost as much as I am.'

'Certainly not as much,' said the judge, 'but I admit I do think about it from time to time.'

'Well, now you can forget it. It's all taken care of.'

CHAPTER TWELVE

Fingerprints?

The commander and his wife issued the invitations and most people, including the Partridges, accepted. Before the day of the party the commander went to see the Chief Constable, whom he knew slightly, and asked him the best way in which he could achieve his object.

'Somebody fiddling the funds, I suppose?'

'No, not exactly that.'

'Oh well, it's none of my business. But I've never been asked such a question before. It's a dinner party, you say. Well, it's quite simple. Give him a longish glass and somehow or other get him to hold it by the bowl of the glass, not the stem. When you take it from him see that you take it by the stem. And of course see that the bowl is highly polished.'

'I'm most grateful to you,' said the commander. 'I hope you won't hear any more about it.'

On the day of the party the commander and his wife went through all the possibilities and decided on a plan of campaign which would ensure that the right glass would be handed to Mr Partridge. But the party had been going on for about an hour and there was still no sign of him. The commander began to be worried. He spoke quietly to the judge about it.

'D'you think he's skipped it?' he asked.

'I do not,' said the judge. Have you never been an hour late for a party?'

'Not often.'

'Well, I can understand that in your case,' said the judge.

'But if he were ill,' said the commander, 'surely he would have rung up, or his wife would have done so. Even if he knew he were going to be very late he might have let us know. The card said "6 till 8".'

'It is now five past seven,' said the judge. 'Why should he come before?'

Five past seven became half past seven and still there was no sign of the Partridges.

'Thinking of going to the police?' asked the judge. 'I bet it'd be the first time you've gone to the police because somebody didn't come to a party you'd given.'

Five minutes later Mr and Mrs Partridge arrived, full of smiles and apologies. He had bandaged hands.

'I'm terribly sorry,' he said, 'but I had a fight with one of Marjorie's new gadgets in the kitchen. It cut up rather rough. I thought of telephoning but I know what a nuisance it is to be rung up in the middle of a party and, as I'm perfectly all right, if you don't mind the bandages, I hope you will forgive us only coming at the end.'

The commander condoled with him and gave him and his wife drinks.

After the party the judge stayed behind after everybody else had left.

'Well, what do you think of that, Bertie?'

'Nothing at all. How many times has he been here before and been given a drink? Half a dozen?'

'At least. Probably more.'

'Well, he didn't have his hands bandaged on those occasions. You might just as well have been going to take his fingerprints then. I assure you I didn't warn him and, if I had, he certainly wouldn't have come if he is Gladstone. He'd be back in the Argentine or wherever.'

'Well, it's a very odd coincidence,' said the commander. 'I thought lawyers didn't like coincidences.'

'True enough, we don't. But that's not to say they never happen.'

'I wish I knew whether there were any injuries to either of his hands,' said the commander. 'That would settle the thing. D'you think I might get the doctor on to it? I expect he goes to Bill Strong. He can't refuse to show his hands if Bill calls on him. Bill could say that he'd been rung up by me as I was a little anxious about him, thought he looked a little pale and that it sounded a worse injury than he said. Then if he positively refuses to let the doctor see his hands it would be highly suspicious, wouldn't it.'

'But you'd have to let the doctor into the secret, wouldn't you,' said the judge, 'if you're going to do that? Otherwise he won't play. And if you let him into the secret it means his wife will be in it too and she's pretty thick with the Bucklands. It will be all round the place.'

'I'm not sure that I'd have to tell Bill,' said the commander. 'I could ring him up and say I wish he would go and have a look at him and then find out what happens. I could go round too.'

'Well, it's up to you,' said the judge. 'But I don't think I'll join the party.'

At that moment the doctor walked in. 'Hullo, Bill, we were just talking about you,' said the commander.

'I came to take a drink off you. Sorry I couldn't come to the party, but I've just had to see your next door neighbour, Partridge.'

'That's interesting,' said the judge. 'His hands, I suppose.'

'No,' said the doctor. 'Something he ate at George's party.'

Normally the commander, who was a considerate host, would have been very upset at the information and would have said so, called his wife and started ringing up his guests to see if they were all right. But he was concentrating so hard on the Gladstone–Partridge problem that he scarcely took in the last remark, and, to the doctor's surprise, all he said was: 'Did you notice his hands?'

'I couldn't very well. They were bandaged. He'd had some sort of an accident.'

'He didn't ask you to look at them?'

'No.'

'What is wrong with him?'

'Oh, food poisoning of some kind. He's been violently sick. So has his wife, as a matter of fact. Frightened they'll make a claim?'

'George is more interested in his hands,' said the judge. 'Did you ask to look at them?'

'Well, naturally I asked what the trouble was but they seemed all nicely tied up and he said they were perfectly all right so I didn't bother. D'you think I should have?'

'It must have been a very nasty accident to have both hands so bandaged up.'

'I did ask if he'd lost much blood and he said: "Only a bit." I took his pulse and his blood pressure and that sort of thing. Nothing abnormal that wouldn't be accounted for by the sickness.'

'Will a Scotch and soda be all right?'

'Fine, thanks.'

The commander gave him the drink. 'You wouldn't like one of these, I suppose?' And he offered a plate of mixed canapés.

'On the whole, no, thanks very much,' said the doctor. 'But perhaps if I were you I would ring up one or two of your other guests and see if they are all right because we don't want to have you all poisoned.'

'Good God,' said the commander. 'Of course I must. What am I thinking of? Elizabeth,' he called.

'Have you eaten anything yourselves?' asked the doctor.

'We never do at our own parties somehow. I ate a piece of smoked salmon. That's all. And that seems to have gone down all right. But I'm afraid there's none of that left. Bertie and I finished them up after the party. That's to say that Bertie had one and I had two. They were quite popular. Look, Bill,' he went on completely forgetting that he had called to his wife and that she had not answered, 'would you do something for me?'

'I expect so.'

'Go back to Partridge and say on second thoughts you'd like to have a look at his hands.'

'Frightened that he won't be able to play croquet again?'

'Something of the sort. If there were any bad gashes they might require a stitch or something.'

'Oh, it can't be as bad as that,' said the doctor, 'or he'd have told me. He's not a fool. But if it will make you any happier I'll go in afterwards. I didn't expect to be this way as a matter of fact. But my partner's on holiday and as I am on duty I was called out because of your beastly canapes or whatever it is. That's why I came and stung you for a drink.'

'Well, come back and have another when you've had a look at his hands.'

The doctor finished his drink and left. The commander at once went out, found his wife and arranged for her to start telephoning their guests. 'You had better not ring the

Partridges for the moment,' he said. Then he came back to the judge.

'Well, what's the betting?' said the judge. 'I'll say ten to one he finds it's a true story.'

'You're on,' said the commander. 'In shillings.'

'You don't show much confidence, George.'

'I shouldn't like to lift ten pounds off you, Bertie. You're always complaining you've nothing left of your judge's salary after tax.'

'That's not true. Some judges certainly aren't as well paid as they were a hundred years ago or anything like it. But by modern standards we have enough.'

Half an hour later the doctor had still not returned.

'It looks as though you've lost your bet,' said the judge.

'I'm inclined to agree,' said the commander. 'But where does that leave us? Where we started. I still haven't got his fingerprints.'

'You might have asked Bill to get them.'

'Some form of treatment to the injured fingers, d'you mean? Take his fingerprints in iodine. A bit drastic, I think.'

Ten minutes later the doctor came back. 'Sorry to have been so long,' he said. 'That fellow Partridge is a very interesting chap, you know. We've been talking about crime and his knowledge of the subject is fascinating. He ought to write a book.'

'What about his hands? Did you have a look at them?'

'I did, as a matter of fact, but he didn't want me to. Indeed, if you hadn't been so pressing I wouldn't have done it.'

'What did you find?'

'What I expected. They were cut about a bit.'

'Badly?'

'No, nothing very serious. They were quite right. They were perfectly able to deal with it themselves.'

'How many cuts?' asked the judge. 'Were all the fingers involved?'

'I don't think so,' said the doctor. 'Several of them.'

'Was it necessary to bandage both hands?' asked the commander.

'No. Not essential. If he'd had three or four finger stalls that would have done just as well, I suppose.'

'Suppose they hadn't any finger stalls?'

'Then it was better to bandage them up.'

'How d'you think the accident happened?' asked the commander.

'I don't know. Just one of these kitchen gadgets that his wife has got, he told me. I didn't bother to go into details.'

'What George is really asking you,' said the judge, 'is could the wounds have been self-inflicted?'

'Could the wounds have been self-inflicted?' repeated the doctor. 'What on earth do you mean?' And he looked at the commander.

'I didn't ask the question,' said the commander.

'But you would have liked to,' said the judge. 'What is the answer?'

'Well, if he went suddenly mad and started lashing about his fingers with a knife – yes, he could have done it all. But personally I wouldn't have found it much fun myself. My recollection is that some of the heathen in the Bible used to cut themselves with knives to try and persuade their god to perform a miracle or to indicate his presence in some way. But I don't think Partridge is that sort of chap somehow.'

'Is he in much pain, d'you think?'

'Nothing special. If you've ever cut your hands you know what it feels like. And provided it doesn't go bad, there's nothing in it.'

'When will he be fit to play croquet again?'

'He could play now if he had finger stalls. I don't play the game, but he might not have such a good grip. He wouldn't in fact. But I don't know how hard you grip the mallet. That's what you're worried about, is it? Is there some kind of tournament coming on?'

'Oh no,' said the judge. 'Our interest is nothing to do with croquet. But he's George's next door neighbour and he naturally feels concerned about him. He was an hour and a half late for the party as a result. What aspects of crime did you discuss?'

'Oh, a good many. I take an unhealthy interest in prisons and he was able to tell me quite a lot. He's been there himself of course often.'

'As a probation officer, you mean, or a visitor?'

'Of course.'

'Would you say he was on the side of the criminal or the State?'

'Both, I should think. He doesn't like people being locked up but he sees no alternative if they're a danger to the State. Nor do I.'

'He didn't happen to mention that fellow Gladstone, the bank robber who escaped?'

'He did, as a matter of fact. Actually that's one of the reasons I'm late. He turned on the news. He said he wanted to hear if they'd caught him.'

'Did they mention him?'

'No, not a word.'

'How did he come to mention Gladstone?'

'I'm not sure. I think I did first. We were talking about big shots in crime. I think I said I wouldn't like to be in his shoes. Never knowing when my last moment of freedom had come.'

'What did he say?'

'He said: "Oh, I don't suppose he'd worry over much. These chaps take life as it comes. They make the best of it while they're outside prison and the best of it when they're inside. Of course they try not to get inside."'

'And when they're inside,' said the judge, 'they try to get outside. On this occasion very successfully, it seems. How reluctant was he to let you remove the bandages?'

'Reluctant isn't quite the word. He said he didn't want to put me to the trouble when it wasn't necessary.'

'You say he could have managed with finger stalls,' said the judge. 'Would a bit of Elastoplast have been just as good?'

'Yes, come to think of it,' said the doctor. 'If he'd got enough Elastoplast in the house that would have done very well. Personally I should prefer it. It gives you more freedom.'

'Did you ask if he'd got any?'

'I didn't, as a matter of fact. D'you want me to go back and do so? I'm beginning to wonder what all this is about?'

'He's pretty well-to-do,' said the commander. 'He didn't by any chance tell you how he made his money?'

'He did not,' said the doctor. 'And I didn't ask him. I'm a doctor. Not a private investigator. But it looks to me as though I'm being used as one.'

'In a way you have been,' said the judge. 'I don't think it's fair not to say, George.'

'It's up to you, Bertie,' said the commander. 'You're the person who's frightened of rumours being spread around.'

'You're not suggesting that I spread rumours around?' said the doctor a little indignantly.

'Certainly not,' said the judge. 'This is rather a delicate matter and the fewer people who know it the better.'

'The fewer people who know what? Is there something wrong with Partridge?'

'The truth of the matter is,' said the judge, 'that we don't know. I don't think there is but George is very doubtful about it.'

And they then told the doctor what had been happening.

'Good gracious,' said the doctor, 'what a thrill for the neighbourhood if it were true. It would put Little Bacon on the map.'

'Well, now you've heard everything,' said the judge. 'What's your view, Bill?'

'I'd certainly take his fingerprints if I could get them. But then I suppose it's different for me. I'm so often meeting people in two capacities. One, the friend, and two, the patient. And I'd have no hesitation whatever in going to the police if I suspected there was something wrong.'

'Well, go,' said the commander.

'D'you mean me go to the police?'

'Well, that's what you said.'

'Why don't you?'

'We feel awkward about it. You say you wouldn't mind. Then why don't you go?'

'What would I say?'

'Simply that there's a chap in the neighbourhood whom some people think may be Gladstone. Tell them to go and have a dekko. They needn't say you told them.'

'But we come back to the same thing,' said the judge. 'He'd know that one of us had done so. Whether it's the parson or the doctor or you or me, it doesn't really matter.

I don't think it's on. You'll have to wait for his hands to heal and then take his fingerprints.'

'How long will that be?' said the commander.

'About a week or ten days, I suppose.'

'Will there be scars to affect the fingerprints?'

'I shouldn't think so for a moment.'

'Would you get fingerprints on a croquet mallet, d'you think?'

'I'm not an expert,' said the doctor. 'I haven't the faintest idea. The police could tell you. I tell you what. You could put some sticky stuff on the mallet. That should take the prints and when he complains about the mallet being sticky you could take it away from him and apologise and give him another.'

'Suppose he didn't say anything?'

'If you make it sticky enough, he's bound to. He couldn't play with it.'

'Not a bad idea,' said the commander. 'We'll fix up a match in ten days' time.'

CHAPTER THIRTEEN

The Sticky Mallet

Ten days later the match took place. Partridge said nothing at first when he was given the mallet but after he'd played a shot or two: 'Whose idea was this?' he asked.

'Idea?' queried the commander innocently.

'This Gripfix stuff or whatever it is. I think it's jolly good. The only thing is that I hate having my hands sticky. It comes from childhood as a matter of fact. When I was too young to complain, on one occasion they didn't wipe the jam off my hands or face. I can always remember the frustration. Ever since then I've always wanted to wash my hands if there's anything sticky on them. And usually if I eat a melon or a grapefruit I need a finger-bowl.'

'I'm so sorry,' said the commander. 'I'll get you another mallet.'

'No, I like this one. I'll just wipe it off with a rag if you'll let me have one.'

'Oh, that would be a nuisance,' said the commander.

'Not at all,' said Partridge. 'I've played with this one before. It's just the right weight and the right grip. So if you'll just let me have a rag, I'll wipe it all off. Or I'll go into the kitchen and do it, if you don't mind.'

There was nothing for it. Partridge had to be allowed to clean the mallet. Subsequently he beat the commander by fifteen points.

'Sorry about that,' he said. 'I'm afraid I'm too good this afternoon. You'll get your revenge next time.'

'I doubt it,' said the commander. 'You're too good for us. Where did you learn?'

'I never learned. I just picked it up. I've got quite a good eye. And the most important thing in croquet is thinking ahead. Given reasonable skill the player with the best brain will win. "If I do this and fail, what will he be able to do to me? Not much?" Then it's worth the risk. It's the same in life really. The chap who gets on is the chap who thinks ahead. But the judge must know that. The lawyers are doing it the whole time. Particularly in cross-examination.'

'Have you ever been cross-examined?' asked the commander.

'Not in court. But like most strangers in a new district I was cross-examined pretty severely when I first came here. Not least, if I may say so, by you and the judge. I hope I gave a satisfactory account of myself.'

'Couldn't have been better,' said the commander.

'That's a comfort. The most frustrating thing in the world must be to tell the truth and not to be believed. That's a thing that's always worried me. I *remember reading the story of Cassandra when I was a small boy. You know. The Trojan prophetess who was cursed with the fate to prophesy the truth and never to be believed. I was horrified by the story. It gave me claustrophobia and I remember working out, even then, even at that age, that the only sure way of always being believed was always to tell the truth. And by and large I must say that people have believed me.'

'There's a lot in what you say,' said the commander. 'And about this thinking ahead business too. We always do it in the Navy. Everyone has to do it. And the chap who thinks ahead fastest always wins. You're pretty good at it, I imagine.'

'Not bad,' said Partridge. 'But I'm seldom in a position, certainly not in recent years, when it mattered very much. It's just as well. I don't like fighting, except in play. I didn't like business for that reason. You're always fighting someone. Either your competitors or your customers or the bank or the tax people.'

'You fight all right at croquet,' said the commander. 'Oh, that's play, and it's very pleasant when nothing hangs on it.'

'Or,' said the commander, 'when you know you're going to win.'

'That's true,' said Partridge. 'I am a pretty confident chap, I suppose. Dangerous, of course. Too much self-confidence has ruined a good many people. All the same, you've got to be confident if you're going to do anything. If you don't believe in yourself, who is going to believe in you. What a nice chap the doctor is, don't you think?'

'Yes, we're all very fond of him.'

'And terribly helpful. The way he insisted on coming round and looking at my hands the other day. How many doctors d'you think would have done that?'

'Quite frankly,' said the commander, 'I think some of them would have looked at them when they first came round to see you.'

'I was bellyaching, literally, too much about other things for him to worry about my hands. I'm sorry to remind you of it. I'm so glad that nobody else was affected. I wonder what it was.'

'Just one of those things,' said the commander. 'But we're terribly sorry about it, and so very glad it was no worse.'

'Oh, it was nothing,' said Partridge. 'We were perfectly all right the next day. Both of us.'

'It was bad luck having both accidents on the same day.'

'If nothing worse ever happens to us we shan't do badly.'

CHAPTER FOURTEEN

The Deputation

While the commander was being beaten at croquet and failing to get Partridge's fingerprints, the judge, on his way home from court after an early day, was doing what he had told the commander not to do – thinking about Partridge, occasionally about Partridge's wife, and finally of his own duty. A judge has to act more responsibly in his private life than most other people. In the United States they have long codes of ethics as to how judges are to behave in their private lives, both financially and socially and otherwise. This is in addition to the code of conduct required of a judge in his judicial capacity. He is told, for example, that he should exhibit an industry and application commensurate with the duties imposed upon him. He is also advised that it is improper for him to accept a loan from a lawyer on a second mortgage which has no investment value. It is improper for him to conduct a newspaper column of comment on current news items and matters of general interest. He should not allow his private affairs or private interests to interfere with his prompt and proper performance of his judicial duties. But the behaviour of English judges is regulated by tradition and, although it is true to say that very occasionally an English judge will break one of the rules laid down for his

American brethren, most judges instinctively know how to behave. Two things must be remembered. First, as far as English judges are concerned, it is only when they don't behave, that mention is made of their behaviour in the press. And, secondly, as regards American judges, they have not yet had two hundred years of judging. It is very doubtful if English judges were any better than American judges, say, eight hundred years ago. So there is no reason for English lawyers to be patronising in the matter.

The first thing that the judge considered on his way home was whether he ought to go to the Lord Chancellor's Department and put the problem to them. But what could they say to him? They could offer to refer the matter to the police themselves, but this would mean the police visiting Partridge and questioning him and then he'd be bound to know that the probability was that this was initiated by somebody in the neighbourhood. The judge had one great virtue. He never solicited advice in order to shelve his own responsibility. He did from time to time, like most people, ask advice, not because he was prepared to take it but because he wanted to think the matter out and the easiest way of doing it was to talk to somebody about it and so find out what his own views really were. If it were a matter of pure law he would be perfectly prepared to change his view of the matter if he thought he should do so. But he would never seek to avoid personal responsibility. In the Armed Services and the Civil Service it is not unknown for a person to do something in order that he should be "covered". Many commanding officers must have said to their adjutants: 'I think we'll be "covered" if we do that.'

Judge Ward had a duty not only as an ordinary citizen but as a Circuit judge. Circuit judges are higher in the legal hierarchy than County Court judges were, but they are still only moderately placed. Supposing it turned out that after all the escaped bank robber was living in Little Bacon within half a mile of a Circuit judge who knew him quite well, people might say: 'What do you expect of a Circuit judge?' He would be letting down the side badly if Partridge were Gladstone and he had done nothing about it. On the other hand, as a resident of a good many years' standing he would be letting down his neighbour, if he advocated a course which resulted in Partridge being questioned by the police and turning out to be a respectable citizen who had once been brought up in an institution and nevertheless made good in life. All the way in the car he tried to hammer out the arguments for and against going to the police. It was true that another attempt could be made to take his fingerprints now that his hands were healed, but the judge liked this less and less. It was the police's job to take fingerprints. It was intolerable to invite a man into your house and to trick him like that. If he were an impostor the police were the people to inform. Should they be informed? By the time he had arrived home he had reached only one conclusion. That was to call an informal meeting of his neighbours to try and thrash the matter out once and for all. This decision was reinforced after the commander told him of his failure to get fingerprints on the croquet mallet.

So the judge called a meeting of his chief friends in the neighbourhood, which included of course the commander, the vicar, Mrs Winchcombe, the estate manager and one or two others. He considered asking Mr Buckland but decided on the whole that it was safer not to do so. He did not invite the wives, and he asked his own wife to see that they were not disturbed. She, of course, knew all about it but had no particular advice to offer on the subject.

151

Unknown to him some of the wives were having a separate meeting on their own. Their problem was this. They were aware of the possibility that Partridge was not what he professed to be and that one day the arm of the law might whisk him away, in which case Mrs Partridge would get left behind. She was very beautiful and attractive, which did not endear her to some of the wives. But, on the other hand, she was extremely pleasant to everybody and did not attempt to throw her weight about. In the normal way an ordinary newcomer, after having served an apprenticeship of six months or so, if found worthy, would be invited to be on the Ladies Committee of the Women's Institute. All things being equal, Mrs Partridge would certainly have been invited. But supposing it did happen that Partridge was suddenly whisked off to jail and she remained behind, it would be very embarrassing to have the wife of a jailbird on the Ladies' Committee. Yet, unless she were charged with a criminal offence such as harbouring an escaped criminal, it would be very difficult to ask her to resign. Most women would probably have resigned in those circumstances, but nobody could tell for certain whether she would. Eventually the meeting decided that the best course was to postpone a decision and to see what happened in the next few months.

Meantime, the judge's meeting was getting under way. The commander came round to the judge's view that the taking of fingerprints should not be attempted again. No doubt his two failures helped him to change his mind on the subject. As everyone agreed with this, the sole question seemed to be whether the police should be informed or not. When everybody had had his say, the judge said: 'I wonder if it would help you if I tried to sum up the case not only for your benefit but for mine, so that we can try and look at the matter fairly and squarely from every point of view.'

The judge enjoyed summing up. In criminal cases he was fair and prolix and exceedingly repetitious. It is a fact that in an unprepared summing up only the very best judges fail to repeat themselves to some extent. This is probably due to three causes. First, that the speaker wants to be sure that he hasn't missed a certain point and therefore, in case he hasn't said it before, says it again. Secondly, that he may want to emphasize the point, in which case repetition is deliberate and quite justifiable, and, thirdly, because although he has mentioned the point once or twice, he suddenly finds a better way of putting it. There is possibly a fourth reason. Some judges are not very good at summing up.

'I am going to try,' he began, 'to put both sides of this worrying matter before you as objectively as I possibly can. I must assure you that I am talking to myself as much as to anyone and please don't be influenced by anything that I say unless you are really convinced that it is right. Please interrupt me if I state any fact wrongly. If I go too fast, please stop me too. It must sometimes be very difficult for jurymen to follow a judge's summing up which may take several hours or even several days. While they are trying to take a note of one sentence, he is at least three sentences ahead. Most lawyers are skilled at putting down in one or two words the gist of a whole paragraph and certainly of a sentence, but this is much more difficult for other people. So, as I say, please don't hesitate to tell me if I'm going too fast. Now, what are the facts? Nine months ago Gladstone escaped from custody. He is a man of between forty and fifty, height about five foot ten or eleven, with a roundish face, dark brown hair and what I shall call ordinary features. His nose is neither aquiline nor snub nor particularly large nor particularly small. His lips are neither thin nor full. His ears are normal. They don't flap out as I believe the ears of some criminals do and, on the other hand, they are not so close to his head that they almost touch. He has neither a very determined nor a receding chin. His neck seems like anyone else's. His hands and feet seem normal for the size of the man. We have not, of course, ever been supplied with Gladstone's dimensions, but the description of him given by the police tallies fairly well with that of Mr Partridge. By the way, if I sometimes say "Partridge" and sometimes "Mr Partridge", you will understand that this is due to my being a habitual reader of *The Times*. Owing to the unsatisfactory behaviour of one or more judges in insisting upon calling people charged in front of them by their surname without any prefix, *The Times* suddenly took into its head not only that this conduct was wrong (as I think it was) but that *The Times* itself should always be courteous in referring to anyone by name, whatever they may have done. So you will see in its columns this sort of thing, where a man has been found guilty of bestial conduct, including kicking a man's face into the ground: "The judge then sentenced Mr Jones to imprisonment for life." In passing I am happy to say that whatever Mr Gladstone may have done it was not suggested that he was guilty of conduct of that kind. Indeed, I cannot imagine that, if Partridge is Mr Gladstone, his crimes were ever aggravated by violence. George was present when he first came to the neighbourhood when, as you've heard, the first thing he did was to ask for the police station. On the whole, I should have thought that that was in his favour, but I quite follow the argument that he had to get to know the local bobby and therefore possibly the sooner he did so the better. As against that, he really did want some protection as I believe that he really did think he was being shot at. He is not a countryman and he was wholly unaware of the type of bird scarer that I had put on his trees. Well, there it is. That's entirely a matter for you. Then we have the photograph of Gladstone with George's pencilled addition. You have all seen this and it is undoubtedly somewhat like the man, but, as you know, I got George to add a beard and moustache like Partridge's on to a number of other people's photographs and they've become not unlike him too. I think myself the probable result is that, though Partridge is like Mr Gladstone both in the description given to the public by the police and in the photograph as altered by George, many other people could fit the same description. But of course it's a vital point because, if he didn't fit the description, he would never have been suspected at all. He came to us when Mr Gladstone had been free for about six months. As far as I can see the things against him in addition to his appearance are as follows. First, he is obviously fairly well-to-do but has given no one an account of how he made his money. Secondly, he does not appear to have any friends or acquaintances outside the neighbourhood. I must say that I find this very odd. It is quite true that he may be trying to live down some misbehaviour of his in the past or, as Betty suggested to me, some scandalous divorce case, and to start a new life here, but he did confide in me that he was brought up in an institution. If he were feeling in such a confiding mood, why didn't he tell me about the scandal or this other life of his which he had given up? That is only a passing thought, but it does disturb me rather. Unfortunately we have not seen his letters. The postman certainly calls on him, but obviously we couldn't ask him for any information. It would have been wrong of him to give it and excessively wrong on our part to ask it.

The fact that, when George sought to get his fingerprints, he had had an accident shortly before, seems to me to get us nowhere. It is of course possible that somehow or other he thought this might be going to happen, but, if so, why didn't he act in a similar way on previous occasions? If we were now considering whether there was any evidence on which to call the police in, the answer would be unhesitatingly no, of course there isn't. But that isn't our problem, as you know. Our problem is simply whether to notify the police that there is a possibility, however faint, that Partridge is not Partridge at all but Gladstone. I feel that I am probably more responsible than anyone else for deciding whether to take this course or not. And when I have decided what the right course is I shall not personally shirk my responsibilities, whatever views you may have on the subject, although those views will be relevant to my responsibility. What I mean is this. That, whoever actually goes to the police, Partridge will know when the police come to make enquiries of him that there must have been talk in the neighbourhood. And, assuming as we all hope, that these suggestions are ridiculous and that Partridge is as law-abiding citizen as we are, it must surely create a difficulty between us in the future because he will say to himself, will he not, surely if they liked me well enough they could have come to me quite frankly and said: "Look, Partridge, people in the neighbourhood have been talking. We are quite sure that they are talking absolute nonsense but we thought it only right to tell you, so that you can stop these absurd rumours once and for all." "Why haven't they done that?" he would say to himself. I must say that, speaking for myself, I should feel pretty uncomfortable going to dinner with Partridge after he'd been cleared by the police. I think it will be uncomfortable for him, uncomfortable for all of us and it might easily result in his having to leave the neighbourhood. This would be grossly unfair. That is why the problem is such a difficult one to solve and that is why I didn't in the first instance dissent from George's suggestion of taking his fingerprints. I recognise that this could be done without anybody else knowing, that the police wouldn't know whose fingerprints they were and that, unless they turned out to be Gladstone's, no harm of any kind would be done. Nonetheless, I must say I shouldn't have had the courage to do it myself.'

At that moment the judge's wife came into the room. The judge waved her away.

'But dear, I think you ought to know – ' she began.

'Later, please,' said the judge. 'This is very, very important and I am just in the middle ...'

'But, Bertie – ' she said.

'Please, darling, afterwards,' said the judge, firmly, and his wife withdrew. 'Now I forget where I was. Oh yes, about the fingerprints. Well, that's not on any longer. At least I don't think so. So we have to decide whether in fact the likeness, the absence of friends and acquaintances outside the neighbourhood and the fact that no one knows how he made his money justify us or, putting it another way, compel us to report the matter to the police. You must remember that the police have frequently said that any information, however unimportant it might seem, should be reported to them. Unpleasant as the task may be does not the very slight information we have come within those words? I repeat – however unimportant it may seem. We must remember that it is often only by picking up the threads of a story from different people – threads which may seem very trivial by themselves but which put together make up the rope which hangs the man. Well, there it is. I've done the best I can, as dispassionately as possible, to put what seemed to me to be the facts and considerations before you. If I have left out anything, please remind me. If anybody else would like to say anything or express any views, would they please do so.'

'Thank you very much, Bertie,' said the commander. 'You know my views and they haven't changed. I think we should go to the police.'

'We'd better vote on it,' said the judge, 'and I think perhaps a secret vote would be more satisfactory.' He tore up some pieces of paper and handed them round. 'Perhaps you would write a "Y" or an "N". "Y" means go to the police and "N" means don't go. I'll get a hat to put them in.' He went out of the room and found his wife outside. 'We'll be ready for tea shortly,' he said, 'thank you very much. I'm so sorry to have been so brusque with you, but I really was trying to think hard and it would have put me off if you had interrupted at that moment.'

'Well, dear,' said his wife, 'you know best and so I withdrew. But I thought you were talking to them about Gladstone.'

'Well, of course I was. You know what it's all about.'

'Well, it's just come through on the wireless that he's been arrested in Calais.'

'Good God!' said the judge. 'Are you sure?'

'Of course I'm sure,' said his wife. 'I was listening to some music and there was suddenly a newsflash.'

'What did it say? I must be clear about it,' said the judge.

'It simply said that John Gladstone the bank robber who had escaped from custody just after his sentence nine months ago was arrested by Superintendent Beaks in Calais this morning.'

Before the judge had time to go and tell the others what his wife had told him Mary Buckland suddenly arrived.

'I must see you,' she said.

'Well you are,' said the judge. 'You've come to tell us the news, I suppose. Well, I've just heard it myself.'

'You can't have,' said Mary.

'Well my wife did.'

'I don't know what you're talking about,' said Mary. 'I've come to see you about Mr Partridge. I felt I had to tell you.'

'Tell us what?' said the judge.

'Well, I know what you've been saying about him and so I went to him yesterday and asked him if there was any truth in it. He looked completely astounded when I asked him and then he smiled and said: "What an extraordinary thing for people to think of me. I hope you haven't believed it," and I said I hadn't. I do think it really too bad, judge, that you've all ganged up against him.'

'But haven't you heard the news?'

'What news?'

'Gladstone was arrested in Calais this afternoon.'

'And doesn't that make you feel ashamed of yourself?' said Mary.

'I'm not sure,' said the judge, 'but I must tell the others. Come in with me, and come in, dear.'

The three of them went into the room and the judge told the others what had happened.

'It's a great relief,' he said. 'But rightly or wrongly Mary Buckland has told him what we've been talking about.'

'That's done it,' said the commander.

'Well, I thought I had to,' said Mary. 'He was such a nice man. I thought it was so unfair that people should talk like that behind his back.'

There was silence for a few moments. Then the judge spoke.

'Mary,' he said, 'I have a feeling that you half believed these rumours were true and that your object in going to see Partridge was to warn him in case he was Gladstone. Now isn't that true?'

Mary said nothing.

'It's the romantic in you,' went on the judge. 'You hated the idea of this nice man, this nice adventurous man, as you thought he might be, suddenly being arrested and flung into prison. Now that's the truth, isn't it?'

'I suppose it is,' said Mary. 'But how did you know?'

'Just a hunch,' said the judge.

'I thought you didn't act on hunches,' said the commander.

'I don't in court, but this is different. Well, now we've got to consider what we can do to put things right.'

'I've got an idea,' said the commander. 'Partridge has got a good cellar. But it can't have everything. I suggest that each of us should take a couple of bottles of our best and go round together and tell him that we're damned sorry. If he's the chap I think he is, he'll accept our apologies in the spirit in which they're given. What do you say?'

'I think you're right,' said the judge. 'It will be the only way to clear the air and quite the best way. I've got two bottles of 1955 Rebello Valente. That'll be my contribution. And you, George, ought to give up that bottle of Romanée Conti you've always been telling me about. You've been waiting for an occasion to use it and this is it.'

'Agreed,' said the commander.

'Well I've got a dozen Vosne Romanée '59,' said Winchcombe. 'Bottled where it was made. How will that do?'

'Splendidly.'

'I suggest we pack everything into my estate car and go round in convoy,' said the commander.

They all agreed and decided on their respective contributions. The vicar gave his only bottle of Dom Perignon.

They went round and collected the wine and put it in the commander's estate car. When it was loaded it was more like the inside of a wine merchant's delivery van. The estate manager gave some Veuve Clicquot and they confidently expected that Partridge would open a bottle or two to celebrate the occasion. After all, he was a man who'd never taken offence at anything, was always ready to help his neighbour and had never shown the slightest temper even with his partner's croquet. They could not believe that when they showed their contrition, it would not be met at least halfway. Probably he would say that he would have thought the same himself. On the way there the judge said to the commander: 'On the whole, you know, I think it's a good thing that Mary told him. I didn't think so at first. But it's much better to bring the thing out into the open. If he had suspected that we were saying things about him it would have made things very embarrassing if nothing were said.'

'I'm sure he didn't suspect anything,' said Mary. 'He was so utterly surprised when I told him.'

'Then if you hadn't told him,' said the commander, 'we needn't have done anything at all.'

'We should not have known,' said the judge. 'That's why I'm glad it's happened like this. Confession is good for the soul. I think we ought to have a spokesman. I think it ought to be you, George. You're the chief culprit.'

'All right,' said the commander. 'I don't mind. I shan't do it as well as you would, Bertie, but if everybody would like me to do it I don't mind having a bash.'

'I shall be very surprised,' said the vicar, 'if he doesn't reciprocate. I think he's a good Christian and will want to live in love and charity with his neighbours.'

'Well, he certainly goes to church as much as any of us and more than most,' said the judge.

'You're not going to hold that against him, I hope,' said the vicar. 'D'you think I ought to bring it into my next sermon?'

'For heaven's sake, no,' said the judge. 'It will then get into the press and be worse than ever. What we want to have is a pleasant meeting now and forget the whole thing.'

'If he'll let us,' said the commander. 'If anybody had done a thing like this to me I shouldn't be able to resist having a crack at him from time to time.'

'Well, that would all be in good fun,' said the judge, 'and we'll be able to afford to laugh at it.'

They were now very near to Partridge's house. They said nothing more until they arrived. They were feeling a bit nervous. Indeed, they were rather like new boys awaiting a visit to the headmaster's study. Even the vicar would have had to admit if he were asked that he had an odd feeling in the pit of his stomach. They reached the Partridges' drive and backed the estate car up to the front door and opened it.

'You're first, George,' said the judge.

They all stood by the front door after the bell had been rung rather like carol singers waiting to know if there were any particular carol which the householder would like them to sing. It was a little time before the door was opened and then Mrs Partridge opened it.

'Good gracious,' she said. 'Is this a deputation?'

'Yes,' said the commander, 'that's exactly what it is. We've come in white sheets to apologise to your husband.'

'To apologise? But what for?' said Mrs Partridge. 'Anyway, do come in.' She led them into the sitting room and they stood about rather uncomfortably. The commander cleared his throat once or twice.

'Well, it is nice to see you,' said Mrs Partridge. 'Donald will be so disappointed to miss you. He's had to go to Calais.'

HENRY CECIL

ACCORDING TO THE EVIDENCE

Alec Morland is on trial for murder. He has tried to remedy the ineffectiveness of the law by taking matters into his own hands. Unfortunately for him, his alleged crime was not committed in immediate defence of others or of himself. In this fascinating murder trial you will not find out until the very end just how the law will interpret his actions. Will his defence be accepted or does a different fate await him?

THE ASKING PRICE

Ronald Holbrook is a fifty-seven-year-old bachelor who has lived in the same house for twenty years. Jane Doughty, the daughter of his next-door neighbours, is seventeen. She suddenly decides she is in love with Ronald and wants to marry him. Everyone is amused at first but then events take a disturbingly sinister turn and Ronald finds himself enmeshed in a potentially tragic situation.

'The secret of Mr Cecil's success lies in continuing to do superbly what everyone now knows he can do well.'
The Sunday Times

HENRY CECIL

BRIEF TALES FROM THE BENCH

What does it feel like to be a Judge? Read these stories and you can almost feel you are looking at proceedings from the lofty position of the Bench.

With a collection of eccentric and amusing characters, Henry Cecil brings to life the trials in a County Court and exposes the complex and often contradictory workings of the English legal system.

'Immensely readable. His stories rely above all on one quality – an extraordinary, an arresting, a really staggering ingenuity.'
New Statesman

BROTHERS IN LAW

Roger Thursby, aged twenty-four, is called to the bar. He is young, inexperienced and his love life is complicated. He blunders his way through a succession of comic adventures including his calamitous debut at the bar.

His career takes an upward turn when he is chosen to defend the caddish Alfred Green at the Old Bailey. In this first Roger Thursby novel Henry Cecil satirizes the legal profession with his usual wit and insight.

'Uproariously funny.' *The Times*

'Full of charm and humour. I think it is the best Henry Cecil yet.' P G Wodehouse

HENRY CECIL

HUNT THE SLIPPER

Harriet and Graham have been happily married for twenty years. One day Graham fails to return home and Harriet begins to realise she has been abandoned. This feeling is strengthened when she starts to receive monthly payments from an untraceable source. After five years on her own Harriet begins to see another man and divorces Graham on the grounds of his desertion. Then one evening Harriet returns home to find Graham sitting in a chair, casually reading a book. Her initial relief turns to anger and then to fear when she realises that if Graham's story is true, she may never trust his sanity again. This complex comedy thriller will grip your attention to the very last page.

SOBER AS A JUDGE

Roger Thursby, the hero of *Brothers in Law* and *Friends at Court*, continues his career as a High Court judge. He presides over a series of unusual cases, including a professional debtor and an action about a consignment of oranges which turned to juice before delivery. There is a delightful succession of eccentric witnesses as the reader views proceedings from the Bench.

'The author's gift for brilliant characterisation makes this a book that will delight lawyers and laymen as much as did its predecessors.' *The Daily Telegraph*

OTHER TITLES BY HENRY CECIL AVAILABLE DIRECT
FROM HOUSE OF STRATUS

Quantity		£	$(US)	$(CAN)	€
☐	ACCORDING TO THE EVIDENCE	6.99	11.50	15.99	11.50
☐	ALIBI FOR A JUDGE	6.99	11.50	15.99	11.50
☐	THE ASKING PRICE	6.99	11.50	15.99	11.50
☐	BRIEF TALES FROM THE BENCH	6.99	11.50	15.99	11.50
☐	BROTHERS IN LAW	6.99	11.50	15.99	11.50
☐	THE BUTTERCUP SPELL	6.99	11.50	15.99	11.50
☐	CROSS PURPOSES	6.99	11.50	15.99	11.50
☐	DAUGHTERS IN LAW	6.99	11.50	15.99	11.50
☐	FATHERS IN LAW	6.99	11.50	15.99	11.50
☐	FRIENDS AT COURT	6.99	11.50	15.99	11.50
☐	FULL CIRCLE	6.99	11.50	15.99	11.50
☐	HUNT THE SLIPPER	6.99	11.50	15.99	11.50
☐	INDEPENDENT WITNESS	6.99	11.50	15.99	11.50

ALL HOUSE OF STRATUS BOOKS ARE AVAILABLE FROM GOOD BOOKSHOPS OR
DIRECT FROM THE PUBLISHER:

Internet: **www.houseofstratus.com** including author interviews, reviews,
features.

Email: **sales@houseofstratus.com** please quote author, title and credit card
details.

OTHER TITLES BY HENRY CECIL AVAILABLE DIRECT FROM HOUSE OF STRATUS

Quantity		£	$(US)	$(CAN)	€
☐	MUCH IN EVIDENCE	6.99	11.50	15.99	11.50
☐	NATURAL CAUSES	6.99	11.50	15.99	11.50
☐	NO BAIL FOR THE JUDGE	6.99	11.50	15.99	11.50
☐	NO FEAR OR FAVOUR	6.99	11.50	15.99	11.50
☐	THE PAINSWICK LINE	6.99	11.50	15.99	11.50
☐	PORTRAIT OF A JUDGE	6.99	11.50	15.99	11.50
☐	SETTLED OUT OF COURT	6.99	11.50	15.99	11.50
☐	SOBER AS A JUDGE	6.99	11.50	15.99	11.50
☐	TELL YOU WHAT I'LL DO	6.99	11.50	15.99	11.50
☐	TRUTH WITH HER BOOTS ON	6.99	11.50	15.99	11.50
☐	UNLAWFUL OCCASIONS	6.99	11.50	15.99	11.50
☐	WAYS AND MEANS	6.99	11.50	15.99	11.50
☐	A WOMAN NAMED ANNE	6.99	11.50	15.99	11.50

ALL HOUSE OF STRATUS BOOKS ARE AVAILABLE FROM GOOD BOOKSHOPS OR DIRECT FROM THE PUBLISHER:

Hotline: UK ONLY: **0800 169 1780**, please quote author, title and credit card details.
INTERNATIONAL: **+44 (0) 20 7494 6400**, please quote author, title, and credit card details.

Send to: **House of Stratus**
24c Old Burlington Street
London
W1X 1RL
UK

Please allow following carriage costs per ORDER
(For goods up to free carriage limits shown)

	£(Sterling)	$(US)	$(CAN)	€(Euros)
UK	1.95	3.20	4.29	3.00
Europe	2.95	4.99	6.49	5.00
North America	2.95	4.99	6.49	5.00
Rest of World	2.95	5.99	7.75	6.00
Free carriage for goods value over:	50	75	100	75

PLEASE SEND CHEQUE, POSTAL ORDER (STERLING ONLY), EUROCHEQUE, OR
INTERNATIONAL MONEY ORDER (PLEASE CIRCLE METHOD OF PAYMENT YOU WISH TO USE)
MAKE PAYABLE TO: STRATUS HOLDINGS plc

Order total including postage:_____Please tick currency you wish to use and add total amount of order:

☐ £ (Sterling)   ☐ $ (US)   ☐ $ (CAN)   ☐ € (EUROS)

VISA, MASTERCARD, SWITCH, AMEX, SOLO, JCB:

☐☐☐☐☐☐☐☐☐☐☐☐☐☐☐☐☐☐☐☐☐☐

Issue number (Switch only):

☐☐☐

Start Date: Expiry Date:

☐☐/☐☐   ☐☐/☐☐

Signature: _____

NAME: _____

ADDRESS: _____

_____

POSTCODE: _____

Please allow 28 days for delivery.

Prices subject to change without notice.
Please tick box if you do not wish to receive any additional information. ☐

House of Stratus publishes many other titles in this genre; please
check our website (**www.houseofstratus.com**) for more details